'Nothing I c... convince you ... genuine.'

'Are?' The tone was cynical.

It had been a slip of the tongue, but Nicole was past caring. 'Yes, *are*,' she said flatly. 'If you want the truth, I've spent the last twelve months hoping against hope that things could somehow be put right again between us. I realise now how hopeless it is.'

Marcos regarded her in silence for a long moment, his expression undergoing an indefinable alteration. 'I've heard it said that actions speak louder than words. If you really feel the way you say, then prove it to me.'

Heart jerking, she said huskily, 'How?'

'By coming to me tonight.'

Kay Thorpe was born in Sheffield in 1935. She tried out a variety of jobs after leaving school. Writing began as a hobby, becoming a way of life only after she had her first completed novel accepted for publication in 1968. Since then she's written over fifty, and now lives with her husband, son, German Shepherd dog and lucky black cat on the outskirts of Chesterfield in Derbyshire. Her interests include reading, hiking and travel.

Recent titles by the same author:

VIRGIN MISTRESS

A MISTRESS
WORTH MARRYING

BY
KAY THORPE

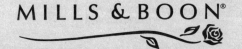

MILLS & BOON®

First published in Great Britain 2000
Harlequin Mills & Boon Limited,
Eton House, 18-24 Paradise Road, Richmond, Surrey TW9 1SR

© Kay Thorpe 2000

ISBN 0 263 81991 4

Set in Times Roman 10½ on 12 pt.
01-0006-49018

Printed and bound in Spain
by Litografia Rosés, S.A., Barcelona

CHAPTER ONE

THE FLIGHT had been late getting in. It was going to be dark by the time they reached Las Veridas, Nicole calculated, relaxing into the soft leather comfort of the limousine seats as they headed for the green-flanked coastal mountains.

'I'm so looking forward to seeing Luis,' she said, tagging on lightly, 'Not that I anticipated such an event!'

'It was a shock for both of us at first,' acknowledged Eduardo. 'Though a wonderful one! Never did I expect at my age to hold a child of my own in my arms again!'

'I didn't expect it at *any* age,' his wife rejoined. 'Having one's first child at thirty-five is no picnic, believe me. I'm still battling to recover my waistline!'

'You are even more beautiful now than the day we first met,' he assured her with the gallantry Nicole so well remembered.

If love hadn't been Leonora's prime emotion at the outset, it almost certainly was now, she judged, seeing the look that passed between the two of them. A year ago she would have said that the chances were minimal, but her stepmother had been a different person then.

A year ago she'd been a different person herself, came the wry thought. Not that Marcos was likely to be making any allowances. The reunion was going to be far from easy, but it had to be gone through. Being there at the christening was more important than any discomfiture she might suffer.

'Who's looking after Luis now?' she asked.

'We have an excellent nursemaid,' Leonora advised. 'She absolutely dotes on him! Her name's Juanita. Venezuelan, naturally, though she' speaks very good English too, so Luis will hopefully be bilingual from an early age. It's going to be interesting to see which one he speaks his first word in!'

'Mamá and Papá are the same in both languages,' said Eduardo, changing lanes to overtake a loaded truck.

'Brother' wasn't, Nicole reflected, wondering how Marcos had reacted to the news that he was to have a baby brother. None too favourably, she imagined. A thirty-four-year age-gap between siblings was unlikely to produce a close relationship under any circumstances.

Coming to terms with the marriage itself had been hard enough for him. Considering the circumstances, he'd had reason to suspect Leonora of engineering the whole thing. He hadn't been on his own initially either, she had to admit.

None of it had any bearing now. The marriage was obviously working; that was what mattered.

As expected, darkness had fallen by the time they turned off the main Caracas highway. Eduardo drove with the confidence of one well accustomed to the winding mountain road, breasting the pass to drop into the wide, tree-studded valley that was all Las Veridas property. Twinkling lights outlined the village, out-shone by the blaze of light from the *casa* itself set against the far wooded hillside. Between, lay the dark swathes of cleared agricultural land that helped make the estate virtually self-supporting.

Bypassing the village, the road wove on for a further half a mile before passing through the big iron gates. Nicole got out of the car to stand for a moment viewing the spacious contours of the Peraza family residence. So far as she could see, everything was the same, but then a year was nothing in the lifetime of a building that had stood for generations.

The man who came to get her suitcase from the car was unknown to her, although that didn't necessarily make him new to the place; she hadn't been here long enough the first time to become acquainted with every member of staff. One short week. That was all it had taken to turn her whole life upside down.

No use dwelling on it, she resolved. What was done was done. Hopefully, Marcos would see it that way too.

Floored in dark polished wood overlaid with an exquisitely worked Persian carpet, the huge hall was as impressive as ever. Paintings covered the walls, many of them portraits of former Perazas. The staircase rising to the upper regions was carved to match the heavy doors that gave access to other parts of the house. Silver glinted from every surface.

Definitely a newcomer was the tall, thin woman dressed in severe black who appeared from the rear of the hall. The housekeeper Leonora had insisted on having, Nicole surmised, meeting the woman's inscrutable gaze.

'This is Inéz,' said her former stepmother, confirming the guess. 'She has charge of all the household staff, so anything you need you only have to tell her.'

'*Buenas noches*, Inez,' Nicole proffered, receiving a brief inclination of the head in return.

'*Señorita.*'

'You're in the same room,' Leonora continued. 'I expect you'll want to go and freshen up before anything else?'

If by 'anything else' she meant facing up to Marcos, she'd as soon it was later than sooner, Nicole conceded. She needed time to gather herself.

'If I wouldn't be disturbing him, I'd love to see Luis first,' she said on impulse. 'Is he likely to be awake at this hour?'

'He's likely to be awake at any hour,' returned Leonora with wry humour. 'Another good reason for putting Juanita in charge. *I* need my beauty sleep. Come on, I'll take you along.'

Their destination proved to be on the opposite side of the inner courtyard from the room Nicole was to have. The same side as Marcos's suite, though probably far enough removed for sound to be contained.

Dark hair scraped back from unremarkable features, Juanita was possibly in her mid-twenties. She greeted them with deference, taking them through from the day nursery, with its bright and cheerful modern furnishings, to a darkened bedroom where the baby lay sleeping in a beautifully draped, heavily carved wooden crib that looked old enough to have seen many past Peraza babies through their first months of life.

'Trust him to make a liar of me!' said Leonora.

'He's beautiful!' Nicole breathed, unable to still a pang of envy as she gazed down at the small face. 'Though so he should be with parents like you and Eduardo. I see the dark hair came through.'

'Skin tone too. The Peraza genes are pretty strong.' Leonora was smiling, obviously in no way resentful of the fact that her son had failed to inherit her blonde, fair-skinned looks. 'I was hoping for a girl myself, but it wasn't to be. Not that I'd swap him,' she added, tucking a corner of the sheet about the child in a gesture more telling than any words.

'You could always try again,' Nicole suggested, tongue in cheek.

Her stepmother gave her a quelling look. 'Once was quite enough, thank you! If I hadn't been careless enough to run out of pills on honeymoon, it wouldn't even have been the once.'

'Couldn't you have got hold of a new supply where you were?'

'Idyllic though they are, small islands in the middle of the Pacific don't boast much in the way of chemists.'

Juanita had retired to the other room. Nicole murmured delicately, 'There are other safeguards.'

'Only necessary, in Eduardo's view, for those in fear of contracting some dread disease, so they were in short supply too.' Leonora gave a smiling shrug. 'Other than keeping him at arm's length for the rest of our time there, I didn't have a choice. Anyway, I thought it would probably be okay to miss for just a few days.'

'Well, something good came of it, at any rate,' said Nicole, eyeing the sleeping baby.

'Try telling Marcos that,' the other responded drily. 'I think he believes it was all part of my master plan to secure my place in the family tree.'

Nicole kept her eyes on the small face. 'I don't intend trying to tell Marcos anything. Not this time. I'm here for the christening. Nothing else.'

'Of course.' The older woman's tone was bland. 'I realise how hard it's going to be for you to see him again, but you've coped with worse.'

She had indeed, Nicole conceded. That final searing

scene was etched for ever on her mind's eye. If she'd been honest with him from the first it might never have happened. There again, if she'd been honest with him from the first probably *none* of it would have happened.

'It would never have worked out, anyway,' she said, adopting a lighter note. 'I think I might snatch forty winks before I get changed. It's been a long day!'

Leonora took the hint. 'Good idea. You've a couple of hours before dinner.'

Leaving Juanita to her charge, they made their way back along the corridor to the gallery overlooking the hall. Nicole faltered in her step on seeing the man who had just reached the head of the staircase, in no way prepared for confrontation this soon.

He looked exactly the same as when she had last seen him, right down to the unyielding expression on the olive-skinned, superbly sculpted face as his gaze skimmed her slender curves.

'Hallo, Marcos,' she got out with some degree of control.

His nod was perfunctory to say the least, his tone even more so. 'Nicole.'

Shades of the housekeeper, came the unhumorous thought. An attitude no doubt shared by the whole household, barring Leonora and Eduardo themselves. The Perazas were venerated by their people. What she had done would be neither forgotten nor forgiven.

He made no attempt to further the greeting, if it could be called that, passing them by to head in the direction of his rooms.

'Men and their precious pride!' snorted Leonora, without bothering to wait until he was out of earshot. 'Ignore him, darling. You're here at mine and Eduardo's invitation.'

'When exactly did you tell him I was coming?' Nicole asked, suspicion confirmed by the look that crossed her stepmother's face.

'Not until this morning,' the other admitted. 'Eduardo had hopes that he'd let bygones be bygones, but Marcos is a harder case altogether than his father.'

Nicole gave a faint smile. 'I doubt if Eduardo would have been all that forgiving if you'd made a fool of him in front of everybody. I don't blame Marcos for the way he feels about me. I played a rotten hand all the way.'

'If anyone was to blame it was me, for making out you were footloose and fancy-free to start with,' Leonora responded wryly. 'I was so intent on getting you married off to a Peraza too, I didn't give a thought to the possible complications.'

'Which only occurred because *I* kept my mouth shut.' Nicole made a dismissive gesture. 'It's all in the past. Let's leave it there. What I'm most interested in at present is a shower.'

'I'll leave you to it, then,' said Leonora. 'You'll be joining us for a drink before dinner?'

Nicole nodded assent, not trusting her voice any further. Seeing Marcos again had proved a greater strain even than she had allowed for. One glimpse of that lean, lithe physique and the memories had come flooding in, riveting an iron band across her chest. No other man had ever made her feel the way he had made her feel—the way he still made her feel. Keeping her emotions under lock and key over the coming days was going to tax her resources to the limit.

As anticipated, her suitcase had already been unpacked. With more than an hour to go before she need start getting ready for dinner there was time to take the forty winks she had spoken of, but rest was the last thing on her mind. Deep down, and against all the odds, she had hoped that Marcos might still have some slight regard for her, she admitted. Judging from the way he had looked at her just now, it was a forlorn hope indeed. So far as he was concerned, she was exactly what he had first taken her to be that day a year ago when he had come to meet her at the airport...

Doing her best to steer a trolley that had a decided mind of its own, Nicole searched without success for a familiar face in the crowd waiting to greet the emerging passengers. She came to an uncertain halt on reaching the main body of the arrivals hall. The flight had been on time; Leonora obviously wasn't. All she could do was wait for her to turn up.

'Señorita Hunt?' asked a voice at her elbow, and she turned her head with a start to look up at the man standing there.

'Yes?'

'I'm Marcos Peraza,' he said. 'Welcome to Venezuela.'

The lack of warmth in the greeting was echoed in the dark eyes surveying her. Nicole tautened instinctively.

'Thank you. I'm glad to be here.' She paused, her glance going beyond him for a moment. 'Is Leonora not with you?'

'Your stepmother is with my father,' he said, still in the same cool tones. 'I was asked to come and meet you.' He took hold of the trolley. 'I have a car waiting.'

Nicole fell into step at his side as he started moving, noting that the trolley no longer seemed inclined to wander. She felt disorientated. Leonora had given the impression that her stepsons-to-be were as eager to meet her as Eduardo himself, but there was little confirmation of it right now. Marcos was the older of the two brothers, she already knew. Thirty-three, Leonora had said.

Stealing a glance at the stone-chiselled profile, she felt her inner tension subtly altering character as she registered the hint of sensuality about the strongly cut mouth. A man of passion when the mood took him, she imagined—a man to be wary of in any mood, her senses warned.

'It must have been a shock for you when your father turned up with Leonora in tow,' she said, tossing discretion aside in favour of a frontal approach. 'I know what it's like to have your mother supplanted by another. I resented it terribly at first when my father married again—especially to someone only ten years older than I was myself—but she made him very happy.'

'It would be advisable,' Marcos replied without looking at her, 'if we left all such discussion until we are in the car and out of reach of other ears.'

With all the row going on around them it would be impossible for anyone to overhear anything the two of them were saying, Nicole considered, but she held her tongue. A long way though it was from the welcome she had been led to believe would be hers, she was not about to turn tail and head for home on the strength of it. Leonora was marrying Eduardo Peraza, not his son.

'How did you know who I was?' she asked, deeming that a safe enough topic.

This time he did look her way, mouth taking on a slant as he swept a swift scrutiny over the mane of red-gold hair, finely balanced features and lithe shape.

'There was no other arrival fitting the description your stepmother gave me.'

Like squeezing blood out of a stone! thought Nicole wryly when he made no further offering. Well, two could play that game. From now on, her lips were sealed!

Parked in a tow-away zone, though seemingly ignored by the nearby official, the luxurious silver limousine took her breath away for a moment. Yet what else would she expect of a family as steeped in wealth and power as the Perazas? she asked herself, unsurprised when the uniformed official leapt forward to swing her suitcase and holdall into the spacious boot. This was probably only one of a whole fleet of such vehicles.

Not that Marcos Peraza was dressed in the fashion one might expect of someone from that strata, his casual cream trousers and open-necked black shirt nothing particularly special. What did draw the eye was the athletic lines of the body beneath the garments: the breadth of shoulder tapering down to narrow waist and lean hip, the length and straightness of leg. Stretched taut over hard cheekbones, his olive skin was unblemished, the thick sweep of black hair above shining with health rather than gel.

Sensing her regard, he glanced her way, one dark brow lifting in sardonic recognition.

'Come,' he said.

She went with him to the front of the car, pulling at the hem of her skirt in an automatic attempt to stop it from sliding up her thighs as she sank into the deep leather seat. Marcos closed the door on her and went round the front of the car to open the driver's door, pausing to pass what looked like a sizeable tip to the hovering functionary.

'No chauffeur?' Nicole asked lightly as he got behind the wheel, forgetting her vow.

'I trust no one with my life other than myself,' he returned smoothly.

'I feel much the same way,' she said with deliberation.

He made no reply to that, lips slanting in the manner fast becoming infuriating as he fired the engine. The meaning was only too clear: at present *she* had no choice.

Traffic thronged the broad highway heading for Caracas on the far side of the mountains. Nicole gazed through the side window, beginning to regret having allowed herself to be persuaded into making the trip. It was obvious from Marcos Peraza's attitude that he was far from favourably disposed towards the coming nuptials. Not that he didn't have some reason, she supposed, considering the circumstances.

Leonora had been on a Caribbean cruise when she met Eduardo. The news that the two of them were to be married had come as a total shock. As her only family, Nicole had to be there, Leonora had declared. Dubious though she'd felt about the affair, Nicole had been unable to refuse the plea.

'You work for a travel bureau, I believe?' said Marcos, jerking her out of her thoughts.

'That's right,' she confirmed. 'A multinational. There's a branch right here in Caracas.'

'You intend visiting this branch?'

'Hopefully, yes. I've been in contact with one of the agents here a few times. It would be nice to put a face to the name.' Nicole paused, searching for the right words. 'Señor Peraza, I—'

'I think in the circumstances we may forget the formalities,' he said with irony. 'You may call me by name.'

The name she had in mind at the moment was a long way from polite; she kept her tone level with an effort. 'In that case, I'm Nicole.'

'I'm already aware of it. You're also twenty-four years of age, and unmarried as yet, though through choice not lack of opportunity. Your stepmother omitted little detail.'

'She'll be *your* stepmother soon,' said Nicole pointedly, smothering her own reservations. 'What will you call her then?'

The dark eyes didn't leave the road ahead, but she saw the jerk of muscle along the firm jawline as his teeth came together. 'There's time yet for my father to come to his senses—to see her for what she really is!'

'And what exactly is she in your estimation?'

'A woman whose interests are entirely for herself. One who would stop at nothing in order to further her fortunes!'

'Such as throwing herself in front of a car driven by a man whose identity she couldn't possibly know?' Nicole kept the sarcasm low key. 'I understood she'd become separated from her party and was attempting to hail a taxi to take her back to the ship when your father almost ran her down. More like the divine hand of fate, I'd say.'

It was Marcos's turn to direct a hard glance. 'If fate played an initial part, your stepmother lost no time in exploiting the situation once she heard the name Peraza!'

'The name might mean a great deal here,' Nicole returned coolly, 'but I doubt if it would have meant anything more to her at the time than it did to me when I first heard it. She was shocked by the near accident, your father kindly took her to a nearby hotel to recover over a drink, they got talking and…' she paused, summoning a half-smile '…the rest, as they say, is history!'

'The rest is not yet certain,' said Marcos tersely. 'Your presence will in no way distract me from my purpose!'

Sea-green eyes widened in surprise. 'Is it supposed to?'

'I believe that is what your stepmother has in mind, yes. Not that I find the idea itself so distasteful. You're not without attraction.'

'Of all the arrogant—' Nicole broke off, seeing his lips slant again and wishing she could think of something sufficiently cutting to wipe the sardonic smile from his face. 'Having spoken to your father myself, I'd doubt if anything you can say or do is going to change his mind,' she supplanted with control. 'He made his feelings for Leonora very clear when he spoke to me on the phone. If you have any regard for him at all, you'll leave him in peace.'

Long-fingered brown hands tautened on the wheel, knuckles whitening under the pressure. 'You dare to accuse me of having no regard!'

'I'm accusing you of nothing.' Nicole refused to be cowed by the tone. 'All I'm saying is, don't spoil things for him. He's found a woman to love at a time when he might have considered himself past such things.'

'Are you claiming that love is *her* driving force too?'

'Why not?'

'You prevaricate because you know it isn't,' he declared hardily. 'Because you're as aware as I am myself of her true nature. She uses her beauty as a snare to entrap the unwary.'

'Which you'd never be, of course.' This time Nicole made no attempt to downplay the sarcasm. 'You see everyone and everything so clearly!'

'You have yet to give me an answer,' he said, obviously not about to allow her through his guard again. 'Do you believe she is motivated by emotion alone?'

'I don't believe she'd marry a man she has no feeling at all for, no matter how rich he was,' she returned. 'Neither do I believe your father fool enough to be deceived by an out-and-out gold-digger. I realise he has to be quite a lot older than she is, of course, but—'

'There are less than twenty years between them.'

Nicole was silent for a moment, absorbing the surprise. 'He must have been very young when he married your mother,' she said. 'When did you lose her?'

Marcos gave her an angry glance. 'We are not here to discuss my mother!'

'We're not going to be here at all if you don't keep an eye on the road,' she returned with feeling as a horn blasted out. 'You almost ran into that truck! I didn't mean to upset you,' she continued. 'It's just that it's the one thing we appear to have in common.'

There was a lengthy pause before he answered, both expression and voice neutral now. 'She died of malaria ten years ago.'

'That's a long time for a man to be on his own,' Nicole murmured tentatively.

'He had no need to be alone. There are many who would have been happy to offer him solace.'

'Obviously none he fancied forming a permanent relationship with. I'm not suggesting that Leonora could possibly take your mother's place—any more than she took my mother's place—but she can give your father a new lease on life.'

'At what price?'

'That's what really concerns you, isn't it?' Nicole accused, shedding what tolerance she had left. 'You're afraid she might deplete your inheritance!'

'Enough!' Marcos spoke curtly, his mouth a hard straight line. 'You go too far!'

He was right about that, she acknowledged. She was doing Leonora no good at all this way. An apology was called for, but she found it impossible to frame the words. Judging from his expression, it was doubtful if he would be prepared to accept it anyway.

They left the main thoroughfare to take a narrower road through the foothills, dropping eventually into a wide, partially cultivated valley where a picturesque little village held a quite magnificent church. The sun was low in the sky when they finally reached the *casa* itself, turning white walls to soft apricot.

Nicole unfastened her seat belt and got out of the car the moment it came to a standstill. A smile lit her face as the familiar figure of her stepmother appeared on the wide veranda fronting the lovely old house.

Beautifully dressed as always, in a suit of lilac silk, Leonora came forward with outstretched arms. 'Darling, it's so wonderful to see you again!' she exclaimed with her customary extravagance. 'And looking so fresh and lovely too after your journey!'

'Travelling first class makes a lot of difference,' Nicole responded, returning the embrace. 'You shouldn't have gone to all that expense to upgrade my ticket.'

'I didn't, darling. Eduardo insisted on it himself.'

Nicole looked beyond her to the man who had followed her from the house. There was a strong facial resemblance between father and son, although the former was somewhat heavier in build, his still luxuriant hair touched with grey at the temples. A kindlier man altogether, she judged, warmed by the welcome in his smile.

'Thank you,' she said a little awkwardly, aware both of Marcos close by and the impossibility of offering to repay the cost. 'It's very generous of you.' She held out a hand. 'I'm very glad to meet you, Señor Peraza.'

'Eduardo,' he said. 'You must call me Eduardo.' He ignored the outstretched hand, drawing her to him to kiss her on both cheeks, eyes sparkling with amusement at her expression. 'English women are so reserved in their greetings!'

'So are English men,' said Leonora laughingly. 'You're going to find everything so different here, Nicole. Wonderfully different!' She slid an arm through one of her stepdaughter's, drawing her towards the house. 'Come on inside. Marcos will have the bags brought in. Dinner isn't until nine, though you can have something now if you're hungry, of course. We've so much to tell you, haven't we, darling?' She directed a sparkling glance at the man accompanying them. 'I'm still reeling from it all myself!'

'I too,' he agreed with an indulgent smile. 'You must regard Las Veridas as your second home, Nicole. Or perhaps even your first in time to come. Leonora tells me you have nothing to keep you tied to your birth country.'

The sudden urgent pressure from the arm looped through hers stilled any answer Nicole might have been about to make. What Leonora was playing at she couldn't begin to imagine, but it was obvious that contradiction was the last thing required.

'Your hospitality is second to none,' she flannelled. 'Especially considering I'm not even a real daughter.'

'More like my sister,' Leonora agreed lightly. 'One I'd have been lost without these last years!'

Nicole let that statement lie. There would be time later to question the motive behind the misrepresentation. Leonora knew she was engaged to Scott. Why she should choose to make out that she was entirely alone in the world was beyond reckoning.

CHAPTER TWO

THE HOUSE was old Spanish, full of archways and alcoves and big dim rooms where the furnishings overpowered at first. Heavy glass doors in the huge *salón* gave onto a covered terrace, with arches leading out onto a central courtyard where a fountain spilled into a stone-walled pool.

Not the kind of home she visualised her stepmother being a hundred per cent happy in, considering her love of all things light and modern, Nicole reflected.

'I'd as soon wait till dinner,' she said, when Leonora repeated her offer of refreshment. 'What I'd love right now is to get out of these things and into a shower—if that's all right?'

'But of course, darling. I'll have one of the maids show you to your room.'

'Why don't you come up with me yourself?' Nicole suggested purposefully. 'As you said, we've so much to talk about. What better time?'

Leonora's expression gave away nothing of what might be going on behind the blue eyes. 'What better time indeed? Eduardo, you won't mind if I leave you for a while?'

'A minute without you is as a lifetime!' came the answer, drawing a laugh from her.

'You're such a tease!'

'I speak nothing but the truth!' he declared with mock indignation.

Still smiling, Leonora led the way from the *salón*

22

back to the hall, moving with the confidence of one already established as mistress of the house.

'Your bags will have been taken up and already unpacked,' she said, mounting the stairs. 'You don't have to lift a finger for yourself while you're here. You might find things a bit depressing with all this huge dark furniture around. A lot of changes are going to be made, I can tell you!'

'You think Eduardo will allow you to make changes?' asked Nicole mildly. 'The whole place reeks of tradition!'

'Eduardo will allow me anything I desire,' came the somewhat complacent answer. 'He's head over heels in love with me. You must have recognised that much for yourself.'

Nicole cast a glance at the beautiful face. 'And how do *you* feel?'

'Lucky.' The complacency was still evident. 'He's an attractive man.'

'That's all?'

Shapely shoulders lifted in a brief shrug. 'It's more than I hoped for. A great deal more, in fact. At my age, love is a luxury. I'm more than happy to settle for what I have.'

'Always providing Eduardo remains under the illusion that you care for him.'

'I do care for him. Just not in quite the same way I cared for your father.'

Nicole swallowed on the hard little lump that rose in her throat. 'Money's no substitute.'

'It has its uses.'

They had reached the head of the staircase. Leonora indicated the corridor stretching away at right angles from the galleried landing, her expression serene. 'This way.'

There was nothing to be gained, Nicole acknowledged resignedly, from discussing the situation any further. Leonora was obviously not about to be diverted from her course. In any case, Eduardo was old enough to look after his own interests. He might even be aware that his emotions ran deeper than those of his bride-to-be, and be willing to accept it rather than not have her at all.

The bedroom was spacious, the furnishings both lighter and less intricately carved than those downstairs. A thickly piled pale gold carpet brought both light and colour to the room.

'You have your own bathroom *en suite*,' said Leonora, going across to open a door on the far side. 'I think you'll find the bed comfortable enough. At least the mattresses are modern!'

'It seems my bags didn't come up yet,' Nicole observed, looking around for them.

'Oh, I'm sure they did.' Leonora moved over to open a door of the huge wardrobe, revealing a row of neatly hung garments. 'There you are! You'll find your wash things laid out in the bathroom, your smaller items in the chest of drawers over there. The bags themselves will have been taken away until you have need of them again. The staff are very efficient.'

Exceptionally fast too, thought Nicole. It couldn't be much more than twenty minutes since her arrival!

'I haven't had time to do anything yet about getting *your* stuff sorted out,' she said, extracting clean underwear from the beautifully arranged drawers. 'It's lucky you rented the flat fully furnished.'

Perched on the edge of the bed, an arm draped about

the moulded corner pole, slender legs elegantly crossed, Leonora looked unconcerned. 'There's nothing I particularly want. Do what you like with it all.'

'A new life, a new beginning?' Nicole queried with faint irony.

'Exactly. Eduardo is the most generous of men.'

Nicole kept her own counsel on that one. 'When do I get to meet Patricio?' she asked lightly. 'Eight years younger than Marcos, didn't you say?'

'That's right. Unusual in this country to have such a lengthy gap between offspring, but it seems their mother had difficulty conceiving.'

'Eduardo told you that?'

'Not in so many words. I think it was an arranged marriage to start with. They still happen even today.'

'But obviously no longer here in the Peraza family.'

Leonora gave a laugh. 'I can't see Marcos being forced into marriage with anyone. He's a very strong character, as you probably already gathered.'

'You could say that.' Nicole regarded her stepmother with purpose. 'He seems to think I might have been brought here as something of a distraction.'

'An aide, perhaps,' Leonora corrected, not in the least fazed. She spread her hands in a gesture meant to convey helplessness. 'I've tried my best to make him like me. You'd think he could at least be happy for his father's sake!'

'Not if he believes you're only marrying him for what you can get out of it.' Nicole paused. 'I honestly can't see how my being here is going to change his opinion any.'

'You can talk to him,' Leonora wheedled. 'Tell him how happy I made your father. I did, you know.'

'Yes, I do know.' Nicole could say that with truth.

'I already tried it. It didn't seem to make much of an impression. Probably because he tars us both with the same brush. Allowing Eduardo to upgrade my seat didn't help. It isn't even as if I can offer to pay it back.'

'Eduardo would be most insulted if you even tried,' Leonora assured her. 'The Perazas are one of the country's wealthiest families, darling! Old money *and* new. Their business interests alone must be worth millions!'

'You really fell on your feet this time,' Nicole felt moved to remark.

Her stepmother laughed, blue eyes sparkling. 'Didn't I just!' The pause was timed. 'You could do the same if you played your cards right. You have everything it takes to turn a man's head.'

'Which one would you suggest I concentrated on?'

'Whichever proves the most receptive. Patricio might look very much like his brother, but he's totally different in character.'

Nicole gave up. It was like water off a duck's back! She said with emphasis, 'I've no interest whatsoever in joining the Peraza family. As you appear to have forgotten, I'm already engaged to Scott.'

'Scott!' The contempt was unconcealed. 'What's he ever going to make of himself?'

'He already made something of himself.'

'Assistant manager of a department store! You can do better than that! It isn't even as if you're really in love with him!'

Nicole bit back the automatic protest, said softly instead, 'Why else would I be marrying him?'

'You agreed to marry him because he talked you into it,' Leonora came back inexorably. 'You know it, I know it, and he probably knows it too. The way you look, you don't have to settle for anything but the best.'

'The best being the one with the most money, of course!'

'Not *just* the money, darling, though it certainly helps. I notice Scott didn't get round to buying you a ring yet,' she added slyly.

Nicole kept her tone level. 'We decided it was unnecessary.'

'He did, you mean. Not that I'm in the least surprised. Stingy as they come!'

It was a waste of time getting angry with her, Nicole conceded. Whatever her stepmother's faults, two-faced she wasn't; she'd never made any secret of her opinion where Scott was concerned.

He'd been totally against this trip—unable to comprehend why she would even consider making it. She'd hesitated to admit, even to herself until now, that she'd needed to get away—to have time and space in which to sort herself out. Leonora was right to doubt the strength of her feelings for Scott because she wasn't so very sure of them herself.

'I'll leave you to take that shower,' said the older woman, obviously deciding to leave well alone for the present. 'You've plenty of time for a nap if you feel like it. It's going to be the early hours British time before you get to bed.'

'I might just do that,' Nicole agreed, with no real intention. 'Dinner at nine, did you say?'

'When it's just the family, yes. Formal occasions it would be ten o'clock or even later. Come on down to the *salón* for drinks first, though.'

Nicole saw the door close on her stepmother in some relief. After the last few minutes she needed some time alone. Scott or no Scott, the idea that she might make a play for either son was ludicrous. If she'd had any inclination that way at all, the very thought of Marcos Peraza as either husband or brother-in-law would have been enough to change her mind.

Sumptuously furnished with sunken bath and gold fittings, the bathroom left nothing to be desired. It was still a little too early to dress for the evening when she emerged. She slipped on a satin wrap and ventured out through double doors onto the covered balcony that overhung the courtyard on three inner sides of the house.

The night air was cool on her skin. Light spilled from several sources below over the paved surface, adding to that provided by the hanging lanterns. The sound of voices floated up to where she stood. They were speaking in Spanish, but Nicole's grasp of the language was good enough for automatic translation, along with instant identification of at least one of the conversationalists.

'I trust neither of them,' declared Marcos hardily.

'You trust few people,' responded the other, somewhat lighter voice. 'Would you condemn Father to spend the rest of his life alone?'

'In preference to his being defrauded, yes. He sees no further than the beautiful face, the tempting body.'

'While you have no interest in such things yourself!'

'A man may satisfy his lusts without losing his senses,' came the unmoved reply. 'The younger one stirs me, I admit, but were I to take her I would feel no commitment.'

Seething, Nicole only just stopped herself from leaning over the carved rail and imparting a few choice words of her own. This Venezuelan egotist wasn't going to be put down by invective. Indifference was a far more effective weapon, she reckoned. He wouldn't be accustomed to that.

Fired by the need to fly her flag high, she chose a georgette dress in muted greens that brought out the colour of her eyes and enhanced the red in her shoulder-length hair. The sandals that went with it were little more than a couple of straps and a narrow heel, increasing her five and a half feet by a confidence-boosting three inches.

She'd show Marcos where he got off, she vowed, viewing her reflection in the cheval mirror. Contempt was a two-way street!

She went down at half past eight, pausing for a moment in the hall to gather herself before making for the *salón*. Of the four people already in the room, only three offered greetings when she entered. Marcos simply carried on pouring drinks at a huge silver-inlaid cabinet, lean and muscular in tautly fitting dark trousers and white silk shirt.

Displaying the same sculpted bone structure, the younger man came forward without hesitation to take her by the shoulders and kiss her on both cheeks as his father had done before him.

'*Bienvenido!*' he said, switching to English to add admiringly, 'You are even more beautiful than I was led to believe!'

'It's said to be all in the eye of the beholder,' Nicole answered tongue-in-cheek, responding to the wicked sparkle. 'Nice to meet you, Patricio.'

'What will you have to drink?' asked Marcos, bringing across the glasses already poured to where his father and Leonora sat together on a vast sofa.

'Oh, gin and tonic, please,' she said without looking his way.

'Ice and lemon?'

'Fine.'

Patricio slid a hand beneath her arm to lead her over to one of the sofas set across the other side of the wide stone fireplace, seeing her comfortably settled then taking a seat close at her side. The sardonic look Marcos rested on the pair of them when he brought their drinks over was a stimulus in itself. Nicole took the glass with a bare word of thanks, her attention wholly on the younger man—although she couldn't have repeated a word he was saying at the moment.

'I offer a toast to the providence that brought this occasion about!' declared Eduardo expansively as his elder son took a seat himself.

'Me too.' Leonora squeezed the hand covering hers. 'I consider myself the most fortunate woman in the world!'

He raised her hand to his lips, the adoration in his eyes plain for all to see. 'It is I who am the fortunate one!'

Nicole shot a surreptitious glance Marcos's way, unsurprised to see a slight curl at the corner of the strong mouth. It had to be obvious even to him that, short of getting rid of Leonora altogether, there was no way he was going to stop the marriage from taking place.

'With barely a week to go, I imagine wedding plans are pretty well advanced by now,' she said with deliberation. 'Is it to be in church?'

'Of course,' Eduardo answered, obviously surprised that the matter might be in any doubt. 'A marriage must be properly blessed.'

So far as Nicole knew, her stepmother had never been a churchgoer, though that didn't necessarily make her an atheist.

'Of course,' she echoed. 'In Caracas?'

Eduardo shook his head. 'We would never be forgiven were we to shun Los Barrancos on such an occasion. It will be a day of festivity for all.'

Los Barrancos, Nicole assumed, was the village they'd passed by on the way here. As probably the main landowners in the vicinity, the Perazas were no doubt held in some esteem by the local populace.

'At least we don't have to worry about having everything ruined by the weather,' said Leonora. 'It's a wonderful country altogether, darling. You must see as much of it as you can while you're here. Perhaps Marcos can be persuaded to fly you up into the highlands to see the famous Angel Falls. He has his own plane.'

'I'm sure Marcos has better things to do with his time than run tourist trips,' Nicole said dismissively.

'Nothing so vital that I must refuse,' came the smooth response from the man in question. 'The Falls are best seen from the air.'

And the feet are best kept firmly on the ground, she thought. 'It's very kind of you,' she murmured, with no intention of accepting the offer.

The dark head inclined, expression incalculable. 'The least I can do.'

'I have no licence to fly, but I'm available to drive you anywhere you wish to go,' declared Patricio. 'Caracas is less than an hour away by road.'

'I doubt that your driving skills will meet the necessary standard,' Marcos said drily before Nicole could reply. 'Mine came under severe criticism within minutes of leaving the airport.'

'I accused you of not paying enough attention to the road, not of being unable to handle the car,' she re-

sponded without particular inflection. 'My fault, anyway, for distracting you.'

He studied her for a brief moment before replying.
'As you have business to conduct in the city, it would
obviously be more convenient to have your own transport. There are a number of vehicles to choose from.'

'I'm afraid I forgot to bring my licence,' she lied,
without giving herself time to think about it, resenting
his autocracy. The smile she turned on Patricio brought
an answering light to the dark eyes. 'I'm sure I'll be
perfectly safe with you.'

'Completely,' he promised.

'What's this about business?' queried Leonora.

'I thought I might visit the local branch, that's all.'
Nicole was already regretting the loss of the indepen-
dence Marcos had offered her. It had been an idiotic
thing to say, an even more idiotic reason for saying it!

She could feel him watching her—feel the telltale
warmth rising in her cheeks; she never had been a good
liar. That licence was going to burn a hole in her wal-
let!

'We can go to Caracas tomorrow,' said Patricio.

'Nicole has seen nothing as yet of the *estancia*,' his
father cut in.

'Which I'd very much like to do,' she claimed. 'Do
you keep any livestock?'

'There are stables for several horses,' he confirmed.
'Do you ride?'

'Not with any great expertise.'

'Then now is the time to gain experience. Leonora
has an excellent seat!'

'I didn't bring any riding gear,' she said.

'We're both size twelve and a five shoe, so you can
borrow some of mine,' declared Leonora. 'You'll enjoy

it, darling. Patricio would be delighted to accompany you, I'm sure.'

'Of course!' declared the young man in question.

Marcos made no comment, but his expression spoke volumes. If she'd had any interest at all in following through on Leonora's suggestion, she'd have abandoned the idea here and now, Nicole reflected, meeting the hard dark eyes and reading the message contained there. No way would he be sitting by while his brother made the same mistake his father was making. She had been warned.

Served in the smaller of the two *comedors*, the meal proved surprisingly simple. The multi-coursed repast she had been expecting was probably reserved for more formal occasions, Nicole guessed thankfully. Adjusting to eating at this hour was difficult enough without being overfaced.

Patricio had taken a seat next to her, leaving her face to face with Marcos across the table. Every time she raised her eyes it was to meet his gaze, though there was no telling what his thoughts might be. 'Were I to take her', he'd said earlier—as if there was no question that should he set his mind to it there could be no failure. Just let him try! she thought hardily.

It was gone eleven before anyone showed any inclination to retire from the table, and even then only to adjourn to the *salón* for coffee and brandy. Nicole took a seat as far away from Marcos as she could get, though with Patricio still in close attention.

She hadn't lingered long enough earlier to hear his response to that last cynical statement of his brother's, though his prior support for his father hardly indicated a common perspective. He came across as a lightweight, fun-loving individual, probably not averse to a bit of philandering where the opportunity offered, but unlikely to prove a problem.

Hard as she tried to concentrate her attention on Patricio, she found it impossible to remain indifferent to Marcos's presence. She could see his lean length on the periphery of her vision—feel the regard that rarely shifted from her. She might not like him, but there was no denying the physical effect he had on her. She could only hope it didn't show.

With the time difference beginning to tell on her, she was relieved when a general move was made towards retirement around midnight. In the morning, Patricio stated, taking his leave of her with open reluctance, he would show her over the estate himself.

There was still no reading Marcos's thoughts when he said goodnight. If it weren't for what she'd overheard earlier, she'd have no idea of his inclinations, Nicole acknowledged. She knew a sudden reckless urge to play him up a little, just for the hell of it, but common sense held the upper hand. She had neither the experience nor the nerve to play that kind of game, not with someone like Marcos Peraza.

Convinced though she was that she had given nothing of the sensations he aroused in her away, the knock on her door some few minutes after she'd reached the bedroom caused her pulses to race. She let out pent-up breath in an audible sigh when Leonora slipped into the room.

'Who did you think it was?' enquired the newcomer slyly, registering the expression on her stepdaughter's face. 'Or should I say who did you *hope* it might be?'

'Don't be disgusting!' Nicole snapped back, and saw the beautifully shaped eyebrows arch in simulated surprise.

'There's nothing disgusting about wanting a man, darling—or in his wanting you, for that matter. It was obvious from the moment you and Patricio set eyes on one another that the fires had been well and truly lit. The days when women were supposed to control their urges are long gone. I was in Eduardo's arms within two hours of our meeting.'

'Would you have gone that far with someone less rich?' Nicole asked, looking more to change the subject than in expectation of an affirmative answer.

Leonora lifted her shoulders, in no way put out by the implication. 'Perhaps not. Wealth is a powerful aphrodisiac.'

'You don't feel you're cheating him in any way?'

'Not a bit. I fulfil all his desires.'

'But you don't love him.'

The sigh this time came from Leonora's lips. 'We've already been down that road. What I feel for Eduardo is quite different from what I felt for your father. Anyway,' she added on a brisker note, 'if you consider love so essential, Patricio is a better candidate for it by far than Scott could ever be!'

'Wealth being the governing factor, of course.'

'Not entirely. He knocks Scott for six where looks are concerned too, you have to admit. You almost had me convinced earlier that I was wasting my time trying to talk sense into you. I can't tell you how delighted I am that you changed your mind. Patricio is yours for the picking, believe me.'

Nicole turned the sharp retort trembling on her lips into a laugh. 'Don't you think you're taking rather a lot for granted on the strength of one short evening? He's the type to make up to any woman he comes into contact with.'

'He's also still unmarried at twenty-five, which would seem to indicate that he hasn't found one he considers worthy. You can be the one if you want to be. Eduardo would certainly raise no objection. He already considers you one of the family.'

'He doesn't even know me,' Nicole protested. 'Anyway, I've no interest whatsoever in ensnaring Patricio!'

Leonora looked unconvinced. 'You'll be telling me next that you don't even find him attractive.'

'Of course I find him attractive. I find a lot of men attractive. That doesn't mean I want to marry them.'

'So what does Scott have that makes *him* so special?'

'Something you obviously wouldn't understand.' Nicole was doing her best to remain cool and collected. 'Integrity comes to mind.'

'Another word for dullness,' her stepmother snorted. She viewed the vibrant face before her in exasperation. 'Do you really see yourself spending your best years in some semi-detached with two or three whining kids clinging to your skirts?'

The picture conjured up brought an involuntary little smile to Nicole's lips, humour quickly fading at the memory of Scott's recently acknowledged total lack of interest in children. He would feel differently over one of his own, she'd reasoned at the time, but it had been added fuel to the doubts already implanted. A marriage wasn't complete without children.

'Starting to see things my way after all?' asked Leonora slyly.

'Not a bit.' Nicole shook herself out of the despondency. 'I was thinking I must give Scott a call tomorrow. At least let him know I arrived safely.' She waited a moment, lifting her brows as her stepmother continued to stand there. 'Was there something else you wanted to say?'

Leonora sighed again and shook her head. 'Time I went, anyway. Eduardo will be thinking I deserted him.'

She moved back to the door, pausing to add, 'I really would think twice about it all. You're never going to have another chance like it. Anyway, sleep well, darling.'

'Like a top,' Nicole assured her, doubting it. A strange bed and a restless mind were enough to keep anyone awake.

CHAPTER THREE

TWENTY-TWO hours on the go proved her wrong on that score. She came out of a dreamless sleep at seven to find herself physically rested, if still with the same circulating uncertainties.

The climate here was wonderful, she acknowledged, getting up to open the slatted door shutters on bright sunlight and a temperature to warm the coldest heart. Wakening each morning to this would certainly be no great hardship.

She cut off the thought before it could go any further, turning back to take cotton trousers and a bright yellow shirt from the wardrobe before heading for the bathroom. Late though it would have been, she should have phoned Scott last night to let him know she had arrived safely. It was already gone eleven back home, and he wasn't allowed personal phone calls at work, so she would have to wait several hours before getting in touch. She could only trust that he'd take the time-lag into consideration and not be unduly disturbed by her failure to contact him right away.

She put her misgivings purposefully aside for the time being.

Showered and dressed, her hair caught into her nape with a tortoiseshell slide, she made her way downstairs to find the *comedor* empty, the table itself bare of all but the silver candelabra and superb central flower arrangement.

She should have realised that the light breakfast preferred in these climates was hardly likely to be served in here, Nicole reflected, retiring from the room to stand for a moment contemplating the options. The area immediately outside the *salón* under the balcony over-hang had tables and chairs ready set. It seemed a reasonable assumption that breakfast might be served outside.

The assumption proved correct, though she was disconcerted on emerging from the *salón* to see Marcos seated alone. He was studying a thick file, a cup of coffee standing on the low table at his elbow. This had to be where the brothers had been sitting when she'd overheard their conversation last night, Nicole judged, working out that her bedroom lay almost directly overhead.

'*Buenos días,*' he greeted her expressionlessly. 'I trust you slept well?'

'Wonderfully well,' Nicole confirmed, trying to ignore the stirring in the pit of her stomach as she met the fathomless dark gaze. She glanced at the two-tier trolley bearing all the makings of a light breakfast. 'Do we just help ourselves?'

'You would perhaps like me to call someone to serve you?' Marcos queried on a note that struck sudden sparks in her eyes.

'I'm accustomed to taking care of my own needs,' she returned with restraint. 'I simply wanted to make sure I wouldn't be crossing any possible demarcation lines.'

'Our people here have no need of unions to lay down the rules by which they live and work,' came the measured response. 'By all means help yourself.'

Nicole bit back the pithy rejoinder trembling on her

lips. Indifference might be hard to come by, but she could at least put on an act.

She took a seat, selected a cup and saucer and poured coffee for herself, tasting it before sitting back in the chair to direct a carefully controlled gaze at the man seated opposite. 'Did Patricio not come down yet?'

'Patricio left an hour ago for Ciudad Guayana on company business,' Marcos advised.

'I see.' Nicole paused, weighing her words. 'I'd have thought the Perazas were in a position to delegate responsibility.'

'There are times when it becomes necessary to bring in the big guns, as your countrymen would say. Patricio is an excellent mediator.'

'Better than you?'

If he noted the irony, he showed no reaction. 'We're not in competition. You need have no fear of being left to your own devices while he's gone. I'm entirely at your disposal.'

'I wouldn't dream of taking up your time,' she disclaimed hastily.

'My time is my own,' he said. 'We'll take that ride together—perhaps even as far as the village if you prove a better horsewoman than you claim.'

'What reason could I possibly have for downgrading myself?' she queried.

Broad shoulders lifted. 'The English are noted for their modesty.'

'While Venezuelans are naturally in no doubt of their worth.'

'No doubt at all,' came the calm response. 'Man *or* woman.'

'Darling, I didn't imagine you'd be anywhere near ready to get up yet!' exclaimed Leonora, emerging from the house with Eduardo. 'It took me days to get over the jet-lag when I first came out.'

'I'm fine,' Nicole assured her, glad to have someone other than Marcos to pay attention to. She smiled at the man at her side. '*Buenos días*, Eduardo. The coffee's good and hot still. May I pour you both some?'

'That would be much appreciated,' he said, obviously pleased to see her making herself at home. 'If you would prefer a hot dish yourself, it can be easily arranged.'

Nicole shook her head. 'This is perfect, thanks. Much the kind of thing I'd have at home, in fact.'

'Then our ways are not so strange to you.'

He saw Leonora settled before taking a seat himself, resting a benevolent regard on Nicole as she handed him a cup. 'You are happy this morning?'

'Very,' she said, wondering why on earth she wouldn't be.

'Patricio too, I think,' he observed, with a smile that set sudden alarm bells ringing.

Nicole glanced her stepmother's way, to be met with a bland expression. She might have anticipated that the idea of a possible further union wouldn't be abandoned forthwith, she thought dazedly. What she would never have expected was that Eduardo might view such a prospect favourably himself—especially when she'd only been here a matter of hours!

It took little imagination to guess what Marcos was thinking right now. She didn't care to look in his direction. Perhaps fortunately, Eduardo appeared not to expect any further response from her, raising his cup to his lips with an air of well-being.

'Where is Patricio anyway?' asked Leonora, obviously not about to let the things slide.

'He's on his way to Ciudad Guayana,' said Marcos levelly. 'On business.'

Blue eyes regarded him in narrowed suspicion. 'Was it necessary for Patricio to go?'

'It was necessary for someone in higher authority to go, yes.'

'Then surely, as the senior, it would have been better if you'd dealt with things yourself?'

The shrug was dismissive. 'My brother is quite capable of handling the matter.'

Don't push it! thought Nicole as her stepmother opened her mouth to continue the discourse, breathing an inner sigh of relief when she closed it again without giving voice to the words almost visibly trembling on her lips. Marcos had enough against Leonora already without her accusing him of deliberately getting rid of his brother.

The idea was ridiculous anyway. Regardless of what Leonora—or Eduardo, at her prompting—might have in mind, it was hardly likely that Patricio's interests lay along the same lines, or that Marcos would have considered that there might be any danger of his becoming so inclined.

She went with some reluctance to change her clothing for the coming ride, rounding on her stepmother the moment they were out of earshot of the two men.

'Just what do you think you're playing at?'

'In what sense, darling?' came the innocent response.

'You know what I'm talking about. I already told you I'm not interested in finding a rich husband. Neither is Patricio out to find a wife.'

'According to Eduardo, it's high time he did,' returned Leonora imperturbably. 'He believes you'd be ideal.'

'You mean you've talked him into thinking that way!'

'I didn't need to talk him into it. He decided after watching the two of you together last night. Patricio, he says, has need of a woman with plenty of spirit to keep him on his toes—or words to that effect.'

'It's hardly up to him!'

'Not entirely, perhaps, but Patricio showed every sign of being well and truly smitten.'

Nicole drew an impatient breath. 'He was chatting me up, that's all!'

'Obviously not the way it looked to his father. Marcos neither, it seems.'

'You can't really believe he arranged a dispute just to get Patricio out of my way.'

'I wouldn't put it past him.' Leonora opened a door. 'Here we are.'

The bedroom she shared with Eduardo was enormous by any standards, the furnishings in proportion. She pulled a wry face as she led the way across to the wardrobes that stretched the whole width of one wall. 'I can hardly wait to get to grips with the decor. Imagine waking up to *this* every morning!'

'Modern stuff would look ridiculous in this setting,' Nicole commented shortly.

'There's such a thing as compromise, darling.' Leonora extended jodhpurs and a pair of shiny leather boots. 'Try these. The shirt you're wearing will do.'

'I want your promise that you'll forget this whole stupid idea,' Nicole declared fiercely, taking the things from her.

Leonora lifted her shoulders. 'I might, but whether Eduardo will…'

'I'll make sure he doesn't have anything more to build on.'

The shrug came again, tinged with resignation. 'Your choice. I only hope you won't regret it in time to come.'

The only thing she might live to regret was coming here in the first place, Nicole thought ruefully, stripping off her trousers to pull on the jodhpurs. Straightening out the situation with regard to Patricio was only half the battle; she still had Marcos to deal with.

Wearing superbly tailored jodhpurs and a plain white shirt open at the throat to reveal a glimpse of gold nestled against dark hair, the latter was enough to stir all but the most resilient of female reflexes.

Hers being far from it, Nicole was bound to admit, feeling the fast becoming familiar contraction of muscle and sinew on sight of the powerful frame. Physical attraction was the devil in that it was totally uncontrollable. All she could do was keep it under wraps.

They traversed superbly landscaped gardens to reach the stable block. The roan gelding already saddled and waiting looked far from docile, tossing his head and snorting when Nicole put out a somewhat tentative hand to stroke the soft nose, his eyes rolling.

'Too much for you?' suggested Marcos smoothly as she made an instinctive withdrawal. 'Perhaps we might find you an older, more passive mount.'

'No!' The negative came out more forcefully than she had intended; she took steps to moderate her tone. 'This one will be just fine. What's his name?'

'He's called Rojo.'

Steeling her nerves, Nicole took hold of the rein and

looked the animal straight in the eye. 'All right then, Rojo, let's get to it!'

Ignoring the proffered assistance, she lifted a foot to the stirrup and hoisted herself swiftly upwards, sinking into the commodious American saddle as the horse took a prancing sidestep. 'I'm here and I'm staying, so settle down,' she told the animal firmly in Spanish, and directed a challenging look at Marcos. 'Ready when you are.'

'So you speak our language,' he observed in the same tongue.

French too, she could have told him. 'Not nearly as well as you speak English,' she said, switching back. 'Shall we go?'

His own mount was a silver-grey stallion standing a good eighteen hands. He swung himself easily onto the saddle, controlling the skittish movements without effort. Man and horse belonged together, Nicole considered, viewing the pair: two magnificent, unpredictable male specimens. It would be a brave woman who took either of them on.

The estate covered the whole valley, much of it still forested, all of it wonderfully scenic. The area cleared to provide a runway for the plane kept in a hanger at one end looked dangerously small to Nicole. The pilot would, she reckoned, have to exercise perfect judgement to clear the surrounding trees.

Once having mastered the gelding's inclination to turn for home at the least excuse, she began to enjoy the ride, although she knew she would probably pay for it by way of a few tender spots the following day.

Apart from the occasional comment, Marcos made no effort towards conversation. Once, his thigh brushed hers as he pulled his horse aside to avoid a semi-concealed hole in the trail they were on, sending a whole wave of sensation right through her. An effect Scott had never had on her, came the unbidden thought.

'If you didn't accept it before, last night must surely have convinced you that you've no chance of stopping the wedding from taking place,' she said, desperate to take her mind off her unruly urges. 'Your father certainly left no doubt in *my* mind of his feelings for Leonora.'

Marcos turned her a cynical glance. 'I've no doubt of his feelings either. Your stepmother is a very beautiful woman. Few men would be impervious to her allure.'

'Counting yourself among the few, of course.'

'Not at all. I find her as desirable as the next.'

Something tautened ominously in Nicole's chest. 'I see.'

'That I *do* doubt,' he said. 'There are many desirable women, but a man has need of far more than that in a wife.'

'Such as a woman born to regard the male of the species with proper reverence?'

'Respect,' he corrected imperturbably. 'An important part of any relationship, would you not say?'

'When it cuts both ways, yes.'

'And you would count yourself worthy of such regard?'

The imputation that he himself almost certainly wouldn't struck deep.

'How dare you?' Nicole exclaimed, and dug her heels into Rojo's sides. Rojo leapt into action and forged ahead of the other animal along the narrowing trail. Unable to exert any pressure via her tenuous one-handed grip on the rein, Nicole clung to the pommel in the certain knowledge that she had started something she didn't stand a cat in hell's chance of stopping—with the horse the least of her worries.

The lash of a thin, whippy branch across her upper chest took her breath. A few inches higher, and it would have been her face that bore the brunt. Whether Marcos was right behind her or had left her to blunder on alone she had no idea. Right now, she didn't much care. Her whole attention was concentrated on simply staying with the animal.

When he started to draw up of his own accord she hardly dared believe it. Fearing to set him off again with any untoward movement, she sat like a dummy until he came to a final, chest-heaving stop.

Marcos arrived as she slid weakly to the ground, the look on his face a timely reminder of the nemesis still to come.

He swung himself down from the saddle in one smooth movement, striding across to where she stood to take her roughly by the shoulders. 'You fool!' he gritted. 'You could have been killed!'

Nicole had never been kissed in anger before. She felt suffocated by the force of it, the pressure compelling her lips to part. Her body squirmed in his grasp. He stilled the movement by shifting to bring the whole of her body into closer contact with his. The musky male scent of him filled her nostrils, mingled with the smell of horseflesh: a mind-spinning combination.

The kiss changed character, lips moving with softer, infinitely beguiling pressure against hers, his tongue a silky caress. She was aware of his arousal—and, even more mortifyingly, of her own. It took every fragment of self-preservation to drag herself back from the brink.

'That's enough!' she managed to get out.

'I think not,' he breathed, eyes fired now by something more dangerous than anger. 'I think it far from enough for both of us!' He shifted his weight slowly and subtly against her, lips widening mirthlessly as she tremored. 'You wanted this to happen.'

'That's not true!'

'No?' He looked deep into the darkened green eyes, leaving her no corner to hide in. 'You'd try to deny what is written so plainly in there?'

'I'm denying that I wanted you to act this way,' she said through stiff lips.

He gave a short laugh and shoved himself away from her. 'The deprivation is as much yours as mine.'

No word of a lie, she acknowledged wryly. Not once had Scott managed to arouse her to this pitch! She was instantly ashamed of the disloyal thought.

Both horses had stopped to graze on the sparse grass beneath the trees. Steadying her nerves, Nicole went to take hold of Rojo's reins and vault into the saddle while his attention was otherwise engaged, dragging his head up with a strength that surprised them both. Marcos was standing where she had left him, the spark still evident in his eyes.

'Do we go on?' she asked, struggling to maintain a surface composure at least.

'The choice is entirely yours,' he said.

'Then we go on.'

He went to mount the grey, indicating that he would take the lead. Nicole turned Rojo in behind him, glad, despite her brave words, of the barrier against any lingering notion on the animal's part to take the bit between his teeth again.

Not that losing control of the horse was her greatest

fear. What she couldn't afford to risk was getting to grips with Marcos again. She could still feel the quivering urge deep down in the pit of her stomach.

Having the object of it in her sights wasn't helping. Broad shoulders tapering down to lean waist and hip, firm male hemispheres outlined by the close-fitting span of material, he left no part of her unstirred. Sheer lust, nothing more, she told herself fiercely, so deal with it!

They emerged from the trees at last, to see the village spread over the hillside, with the winding roadway they had traversed the day before visible beyond. Apart from the one interlude, they had been in the saddle almost two hours; Nicole was aware of a tenderness in the region of her buttocks already, although nothing would have persuaded her to admit it.

Drawing level with the stallion, she stole a glance at the unyielding face of its rider. If there had been any chance at all of conciliation, she had put paid to it, she acknowledged ruefully—ask for it though he had. All she could do was live with the situation. Once the wedding was over, she was out of here anyway.

Back to vapidity, whispered a small, treacherous voice.

A maze of narrow alleys climbing from the main square, almost every building on a different level, every sun-sparkled white wall laced with colourful plant life, the village was a picture postcard. Marcos was greeted with respectful familiarity from all sides, herself with curiosity. Despite its relative closeness to the capital, the outside world obviously hadn't yet encroached on the place. Nicole supposed there was nothing much here to attract the general run of tourist. She hoped for the inhabitants' sake that it would remain that way.

Two of the trio of women talking together on a street corner became suddenly spurred into action on seeing the approaching riders, urging the third member of the group forward. Marcos reined in at the crumbling pavement to listen to what she had to say.

The conversation was too fast for Nicole to follow with total accuracy. Something to do with her husband, was all she could gather.

Marcos hesitated a brief moment, then gave a nod, looking round to where Nicole waited. 'I have to pay a call.'

'That's all right,' she said. 'I'll wait here for you.'

He shook his head. 'It would not be fitting to leave you here alone.'

Nicole failed to see why, but wasn't prepared to make an issue of it. Marcos summoned a passing youth to take care of the horses, then the two of them accompanied the woman to a dwelling a short distance along the narrow street.

A spotlessly clean though somewhat stark little kitchen gave access to an inner room, where her husband sat in isolation, the white cast around his outstretched leg telling its own story.

Marcos lifted a staying hand as the man attempted to struggle to his feet. 'You must rest, José. I came only to assure you that you need have no fear of losing your job because of your injury. Nor will you suffer any hardship while you are indisposed.'

The other subsided, mingled relief and gratitude suffusing his features. 'I am forever indebted, *señor*! You and your lady will take refreshment?'

'Please,' Nicole interposed swiftly, giving Marcos

no time to voice the refusal she sensed hovering on his lips. 'I'm Nicole Hunt,' she added, with a smile that encompassed both husband and wife, sensing also that Marcos was not about to perform introductions. 'I'm here for the wedding.'

The other woman's face lit up. 'Ah, the wedding!'

'Coffee, Rosa,' said her husband sharply. There was a certain constraint in the gaze he switched back to Marcos. 'You will take a seat?'

Apart from the chair he was occupying, and a couple of stools, there was only a worn sofa covered by a brightly coloured rug. Nicole perched herself at one end, aware of Marcos's pinched nostrils as he took the other end. That he was good and angry again she didn't need telling. So what? she thought recklessly.

The coffee was excellent, hot and strong. Nicole took her time over it, drawing Rosa out to discuss preparations already under way for the wedding celebrations. It looked set to be a regular fiesta, with the whole village involved in one capacity or another. The wedding feast itself was to be held outdoors back at the *casa*, it appeared, and open to all.

Neither man made any contribution. José looked increasingly uncomfortable, as if in recognition of his employer's lack of enthusiasm for the coming event. Nicole was sorely tempted to ask for a second cup of coffee, but decided enough was enough for the moment.

Far from helping, the rest had allowed her muscles to stiffen up. It took her a couple of attempts to even get her foot into the stirrup again, while the saddle felt as hard as a brick beneath her cringing flesh. By the time they reached the house she was going to find it difficult to get down, much less walk, she reflected.

Marcos had made no offer to help her mount. He waited until they were clear of the village before letting fly.

'Never,' he said grimly, 'attempt to usurp my authority in that manner again!'

In what manner would it be permissible? It was on the tip of Nicole's tongue to ask, but she controlled the impulse.

'In what way can accepting the offer of refreshment be considered usurping your authority?' she said instead.

'The offer was made to me.'

'Oh, I see. I was supposed to ask you if I might take advantage?'

'It would have been fitting, yes.'

'I take it my introducing myself was outside your code too?'

Her tone drew a dangerous gleam. 'It was unnecessary.'

'Why?' she demanded. 'Is common courtesy only extended to the upper classes in this country?'

Marcos brought the stallion to a halt, holding him on a tight rein as he regarded her with narrowed intensity. 'Are you trying to provoke me again?'

'I'm merely pointing out that I'm not bound by any rules of conduct but my own,' she retorted. 'If you don't like it, tough!'

The intensity increased to savage proportions. 'You will not speak to me in that manner!'

Her own anger had grown to a point where she no longer cared about any possible consequences. Eyes flashing, she tossed the hair back from her face in a gesture designed to express contempt. 'It's high time somebody did! You're the most arrogant, insufferable man I ever met!'

'You have yet to know me in any depth,' he returned, on a note somehow all the more menacing for its relative softness. 'But you will.'

Nicole bit her lip as he put the stallion into motion again, aware of the trembling reaction in her limbs. She'd been carried along by an emotion totally alien to her before this morning, one she didn't care to plumb too deeply. For certain, she had to stop needling the man.

The return journey was thankfully shorter, though no less of a trial. Apart from making sure she was following in his wake, Marcos paid her no attention. Sliding painfully to the ground on reaching the stable yard, Nicole wondered how she was going to get through lunch, much less the rest of the day. It had been sheer folly to attempt a three-hour ride after such a long period away from the saddle.

'I'll have someone bring you up some salts for the bath,' said Marcos, obviously undeceived by her attempt to conceal her aches and pains. 'Stay there for at least an hour. And next time—'

'There won't be a next time,' she cut in with purpose. 'Not in any sense!'

His lips took on the hated slant. 'You think not?'

'I *know* not.'

'We shall see.'

He strode away before she could come up with any response. Not that there was anything much she could have said without repeating herself, she conceded wearily. The morning had been a disaster from start to finish; the whole trip was turning into a disaster. If it weren't for letting Eduardo and Leonora down, she would take off for the airport this very afternoon. With an open ticket she could be on the first available flight home.

To what? asked that small voice.

She made her room without running into anyone, easing off the boots with some difficulty. She had even more difficulty convincing the maidservant who brought the promised salts that she was capable of running her own bath. As Leonora had said, in this household one hardly needed lift a finger if so desired.

The salts turned the bath water pale green, giving off a pleasant herbal aroma. Sliding gratefully into the soothing warmth, Nicole calculated that, with lunch not due to be served until two o'clock, she could afford to relax for a good half an hour before getting dressed again. Hopefully, that would ease the soreness enough for her to sit down in relative comfort.

A fitting retribution, Marcos would no doubt consider it. Looking back over the events of the morning, she had to admit that her behaviour had been less than exemplary. She had never acted that way in her life before. No matter what the provocation, it had been a crack-brained thing to do.

Except that her brain hadn't been engaged at the time. There was even a possibility that he was right in saying she'd wanted him to react the way he had. Reliving those moments when he'd had her pinned against him, she felt the same, muscle-spasming charge. If she hadn't drawn back there was every probability that she would know exactly what he was capable of by now.

And if he had shown her, how would she be feeling

right now? she asked herself, ashamed of the flash of regret. Minus any deeper emotion, sex was just an act—worth no more than a coupling between animals.

To hell with him! she thought fiercely.

CHAPTER FOUR

IT WAS bang on the hour when she made her way downstairs again, wearing the same trousers she had worn earlier, along with a khaki-coloured shirt. Lunch, Leonora had said, was served outside whenever possible. Expecting just the family, Nicole paused disconcertedly on seeing the young woman seated beside Marcos at the table.

'Ah, there you are!' exclaimed Eduardo. 'We were about to come to the conclusion that you had fallen asleep after your bath. Marcos should not have taken you so far!'

'I'm fully recovered,' Nicole assured him, lying through her teeth. She took a seat, turning the involuntary grimace into a smile directed across at the girl opposite. 'Hallo!'

'This is Isabella Laniez,' said Eduardo. 'The Laniezes are our neighbours and friends. You are not too far distant in age.'

But totally different in temperament if the other's present demeanour was any indication, Nicole reflected, acknowledging the girl's diffident response. Not what she might have expected from Marcos's earlier summing up of Venezuelan characteristics. Beautiful, definitely, with her long black hair and huge tawny eyes, the olive skin enhanced by the sparkling white, delicately embroidered cotton blouse.

'I understand you speak our language,' Isabella said in Spanish.

'Well enough to get by,' Nicole agreed. 'Do you speak English?'

'Oh, yes.' She switched to prove it, her accent appealing. 'We are honoured to have you visit our country, are we not, Marcos?'

The 'we' raised an emotion Nicole was reluctant to recognise. 'I'm honoured to be here,' she said with what she hoped was the right degree of lightness. 'It's a very beautiful country!'

'You've hardly seen anything of it as yet,' Marcos put in. 'A matter we must take steps to rectify.'

Not if it meant being alone with him again, Nicole thought; from now on that was strictly out of bounds!

'I'll be happy to wait until Patricio gets back rather than take up any more of your time,' she said, forcing herself to look at him directly. 'He would be disappointed, I think, not to show me Caracas.'

Eduardo laughed. 'He would be desolated! It was cruel of you, Marcos, to send him to Guayana.'

'It was necessary,' replied his elder son smoothly. 'I saw José Rios this morning. He was concerned for his job.'

'He need have no worry,' Eduardo confirmed. 'The accident was no fault of his.'

'He and his wife are very much looking forward to the wedding,' said Nicole with purpose. 'According to Rosa, the whole village will be coming.'

'But of course. The occasion will be celebrated by everyone!'

Everyone except Marcos, she reflected. She cast him a sly glance, to be met by a look that shrivelled her where she sat. Taunting him this way was hardly fair, but she didn't feel like being fair.

'After siesta, I'll show you the dress I'm to wear,'

said Leonora. 'I hope you brought something special yourself.'

'Of course.' Whether her choice of outfit would measure up to her stepmother's idea of 'special' was something else. Nicole turned her attention back to Isabella. 'I look forward to meeting the rest of your family.'

The other inclined her head. 'You will meet my parents this evening.'

'Eduardo's idea—to hold a pre-wedding dinner party so that I get to meet all the right people before the day instead of being faced by a sea of total strangers,' said Leonora, bestowing a glowing smile on the man at her side. 'He thinks of everything!'

From the sound of it, it would be a pretty formal affair, thought Nicole. She took a quick mental inventory of her wardrobe. Apart from the dress she had worn last night, and the one she planned on wearing to the wedding itself, she had packed mostly lightweight cottons and casual gear. Nothing, for certain, that could be considered formal evening wear. As Leonora hadn't seen fit to warn her, she would simply have to loan her something suitable, that was all. It was fortunate that they were the same dress size.

'What time is kick-off?' she asked with deliberate flippancy, earning a chuckle from Eduardo and a curl of a lip from Marcos.

'Dinner will be served at ten o'clock,' confirmed the older man. 'A little later than is customary in your country.'

'When in Rome…' Nicole laughed, drawing a puzzled look from Isabella.

'You are not in Rome,' she pointed out.

'It's a saying the English use to imply that behaviour should be governed by local custom,' said Marcos with irony. 'One many of them fail to put into practice, unfortunately.'

'There are ungovernable elements in every nationality,' returned Nicole smoothly. 'Yours is hardly an exception.'

Looking amused, Eduardo put up a staying hand. 'Peace, my children. Peace! The luncheon table is no place to conduct a battle!'

'Just a minor skirmish,' Nicole assured him.

Marcos refrained from comment, though the sparking amber lights in his eyes spoke volumes. Isabella looked from one to the other of them with an expression Nicole was ashamed to say she found thoroughly satisfying. It was apparent that the girl suspected some deeper undercurrent between the two of them.

It was gone three when they finished the meal. Hungry after the ride, Nicole had eaten a great deal more than was customary for her at lunchtime, and drunk rather too much of the free-flowing wine. She felt more than a little light-headed.

Isabella had apparently driven over in her own car. Marcos went to see her off, while Leonora and Eduardo vanished indoors, having advised Nicole to take advantage of the next couple of hours to rest herself for the evening.

Siesta certainly seemed a good idea, and one of the long cane lounging chairs set under the balcony overhang an even better place to take it. Judging from the silence that had fallen over the place, the staff too took siesta. Nicole didn't blame them. They worked long enough hours.

Inevitably her thoughts turned to Isabella. That she had an eye for Marcos was more than evident. It was his attitude towards her that was difficult to interpret.

More than casual, less than intimate was the closest she could come.

She must have dozed off, awakening with a jerk when someone sat down on the edge of the lounger. Marcos leaned over to grasp the other edge, effectively pinning her where she lay. His expression was disquieting to say the least.

'I warned you,' he said softly. 'I'll take no more of your insolence!'

'What…?' Nicole began, but got no further, the rest smothered beneath the ruthless compression.

It was the morning over again—only more so, his free hand seeking the curve of her breast, fingers splaying to cover and caress. She arched involuntarily to the feel of it, the blood singing in her ears, her mind whirling. Her hands slid upwards of their own accord to fasten into the dark thickness of his hair, her lips moving against his—opening to the silky pressure of his tongue, her whole body quivering at the onslaught of sensation. His breathing had roughened, echoing her own; she could feel the thud of his heartbeats.

Her shirt buttons gave easily to his touch, allowing him access to the warm flesh beneath. He slid his fingers under her brief lacy brassière, drawing a gasp from her lips as he found the aching, tender nub. She wanted to feel those strong lean fingers everywhere, exploring, discovering, possessing…

It took a sudden metallic clatter from the direction of the kitchen quarters to bring her to her senses. This was utter madness! she thought wildly. It wasn't even a full twenty-four hours yet since her arrival in Venezuela!

She tore her mouth free, both hands flat against his chest to push him away. 'Don't!'

'Why?' he demanded roughly. 'You want me to pos-
sess you as much as I want it myself. Why should we
not indulge that need? Perhaps not here, I agree. We
will go to your room—or to mine.'

'We will not!' Nicole made an attempt to push him
further, subsiding helplessly when she made absolutely
no impression this time. The look beginning to dawn
in the dark eyes was enough to daunt the bravest heart,
and hers was far from it right now.

'You think to play games with me?' he demanded.

'It's no game,' she said unhappily. 'Believe me, it
isn't! I was...carried away.'

'And I'm expected to accept that?'

He could hardly do anything else in the present circumstances, Nicole reassured herself. 'I'm afraid you
have to,' she said, forcing a positive note. 'I never intended it to happen at all, much less—'

'You made no attempt to stop it until this moment,'
he interjected brusquely.

'Like I said, I got carried away.' She tried a new
tack, hoping to lighten the mood. 'You're a hard man
to resist!'

For a moment or two he made no reply, gazing down
at her with narrowed intensity, then his expression altered, a reluctant smile plucking at the corners of his
mouth. 'Apparently not hard enough.'

He lifted a hand to refasten the two shirt buttons. 'I
too got carried away,' he acknowledged. 'Anger is a
driving force.'

'I don't mean to make you angry,' she said.

The smile came again, more spontaneously this time.
'Yes, you do. You take a delight in pressing me. So
often with a woman there is this need to test the limits
of endurance.'

'Including Isabella?' she asked.

'Isabella is an exception,' he returned. 'She would never dream of crossing me in any manner.'

Was there just the slightest hint of tedium in that latter statement? Nicole wondered. 'Ideal wife material,' she heard herself saying.

'It would appear so,' came the inconclusive answer.

There was a lengthy pause. Marcos was the first to break it. 'I think we should perhaps begin our acquaintance again.'

Nicole searched the dark eyes for any sign of insincerity, her spirits lifting when she detected none. 'I'd like that too,' she said. 'Better friends than enemies!'

'Friends?' His tone suggested sudden amusement. 'Yes, that would be a place to start.'

'With trust the first requirement.' She kept her gaze as steady as his. 'I'm here because I'm the only family Leonora has, not to find myself a rich husband.'

Hardness returned to the lean features. 'Too, you mean.'

'No, I didn't mean that,' she denied.

'But you cannot in all honesty claim that your stepmother has no interest in financial security?'

Nicole gave a sigh. 'That's an unfair question. Of course she's interested in financial security. Most people are. That doesn't mean she sees your father as nothing more than a meal ticket.'

'But she doesn't love him.' It was a statement this time, not a question.

'It depends on one's concept of love,' she prevaricated, torn between loyalty to Leonora and an innate honesty. 'According to what you said this morning, respect is the prime requisite in any relationship.'

'I said it was an important part.' The hardness was

still there. 'You truly believe she has respect for my father?'

'Definitely. Regard too. Just give her a chance to prove herself,' she pleaded. 'She won't let him down, I promise you!'

'Make no promises for others,' he advised. There was a further pause, his expression set. When he spoke again it was with steely purpose. 'She had better *not* let him down.'

The implied threat sent a sudden little shiver down Nicole's spine. 'She won't,' she repeated, hoping to heaven she was right. 'Does that mean you'll not be doing anything to try stopping the wedding?'

'Reluctantly, yes.'

'And you'll try meeting her halfway?'

Marcos gave a short laugh. 'Be satisfied with one concession for the moment.' He ran his eyes down the supple length of her body, returning to linger for a brief, pulse-quickening moment on the generous curve of her mouth. 'You and I have much to learn of one another.'

'You're going?' she exclaimed in mingled surprise and disappointment as he got to his feet.

'If I stay,' he said, 'I shall be tempted to take hold of you again, and this is not the time or the place. Rest for now.'

Subsiding onto the cushioned mattress as he moved away, Nicole fought against the almost overwhelming urge to call him back. First and foremost she had to gain his respect, and she wasn't going to do it by offering herself to him on a platter, regardless of how much she ached to do just that. His wanting her was only a beginning. If she...

Her thoughts stopped there in sudden dismayed recollection. How could she possibly be contemplating *any* kind of association with Marcos when Scott, the man she was supposed to love, waited back home?

'Supposed' being the operative word, she conceded wryly. If she really loved him there would be no question of whether or not she was doing the right thing. His being the first and only man to strike enough of a spark to get her into bed was no basis on which to build a marriage—and that was about what it came down to. They didn't even have common interests.

She had to straighten things out with him as soon as she got back, she resolved, glad to have come to a decision at last. She was being fair to neither of them in the long run.

In the meantime, she'd do better to let the spark Marcos had undoubtedly lit die a natural death from starvation, difficult though it might be to steer clear of him. She simply wasn't equipped for the only role he would want her to play.

Too restless to even attempt further dozing, she made her way up to her bedroom and the supply of magazines thoughtfully provided, thankful not to meet anyone on the way. The written word proved no distraction either. Eventually she gave up and just lay there on the bed, wondering what Marcos was doing right now.

It was all very well to think about steering clear, but with several days to go before she could head for home the reality was going to prove a real trial. The only hope she had of succeeding in keeping him at a distance was by convincing him that she had lost all interest, and she doubted her acting ability when all he had to do was look at her to start her knees knocking.

The house began coming back to life around five,

but Nicole stayed where she was, reluctant to assume the role. At the very least it had taken her mind off her aches and pains, she reflected, grimacing at the twinges when she moved. She wouldn't be doing any more riding for a day or two for certain.

Leonora came to find her at six. 'Why are you lurking up here?' she asked. 'I had English tea ready and waiting more than half an hour ago.'

'Sorry,' Nicole offered. 'You should have said. Not that I could have eaten a thing after that lunch, anyway,' she added.

'Tea is drunk, darling,' came the dry response. 'I don't bother with the sandwiches and cakes. And it still doesn't answer the question of why you're hanging about up here.'

'I had a bit too much to drink at lunch,' Nicole improvised. 'I've been sleeping it off.' She sought a change of subject. 'About tonight. If it's going to be a really formal occasion, I don't have anything suitable with me.'

'Then we'd better go and find you something,' said her stepmother. 'The Perazas do things in style.'

Going along the corridor, she said slyly, 'You wouldn't by any chance be avoiding Marcos?'

'Why would I want to do that?' Nicole responded with creditable composure.

'The way the two of you were acting at lunch, I'd say there was definitely something going on. Eduardo thought so too. He said he'd rarely seen Marcos so close to losing his temper.'

Nicole lifted her shoulders. 'The heat must have been getting to him.'

'Ah, but what kind of heat? You were gone a long time this morning.'

'Which is another reason why I needed to rest this afternoon,' Nicole claimed, turning a deaf ear to the imputation. 'It's over a year since I last rode.'

'Oh, of course. Scott doesn't, does he?'

With no intention of advising Leonora of her decision until Scott himself had been told, Nicole let the implied criticism lie. It wasn't his fault that she'd allowed that particular hobby to lapse.

The wardrobe Leonora opened this time contained a whole variety of evening garments, many of them recognisably designer wear.

'Some I treated myself to for the cruise, the majority Eduardo helped me choose in Caracas,' she said blithely. 'Along with a load of daywear too, of course. The fashion houses here are top class.'

She took out a shimmering silver sheath of a dress, holding it up in front of Nicole. 'This would look wonderful with your hair! You have the figure for it too.' Like me, the complacent tone implied. 'Here, try it on. There's a pair of silver sandals to go with it.'

Nicole took off shirt and trousers and slipped the dress over her head, stepping into the totteringly high-heeled sandals and turning her back for Leonora to slide the long back zip.

'You can't wear a bra with this,' declared the latter. 'Take it off.'

Doing so, Nicole slid her arms back into the sleeveless bodice and felt the silk-lined garment nestle to her body. The image that greeted her in the cheval mirror was a total shock. High-necked at the front, dipping almost to waist level at the back, the dress followed every line from breast to knee before flaring out a little for ease of walking.

'I can't wear this!' she gasped.

'Why on earth not?' Leonora sounded taken aback. 'You look a million dollars!'

'I feel like…Joan of Arc,' Nicole claimed, and drew a laugh.

'The last thing anyone's going to want to do to you is burn you at the stake! Anyway, it's about time you realised your potential. The only pity is that Patricio isn't going to be here to see it—thanks to that brother of his!'

'No one is going to see it,' Nicole declared purposefully, 'because I'm not going to be wearing it. Can't you find me something a little less…? Well, a little less, that's all.'

'No, I can't.' Leonora had her intransigent face on. 'It's this or nothing.'

Nicole jutted her own chin. 'Then I'll wear what I had on last night.'

'No, you won't. Eduardo would be mortified!'

'You mean *you* would.'

'All right, then, so *I* would. These people are out of the top drawer, darling. I've no intention of having them think I'm anything other myself. If you won't wear what I choose for you, you'll just have to pretend you're indisposed, that's all.'

'All right, so I'll do that,' Nicole retorted angrily, resenting the suggestion that she wasn't fit to be seen in her own clothing.

'Darling!' Both tone and expression underwent a sudden transformation. 'Don't be like this! Eduardo is so looking forward to introducing the two of us to his friends. You look beautiful. You know you do! Why are you so reluctant to show yourself?'

Primarily because she hesitated to give Marcos any further inducement, Nicole could have told her. The dress was a come-on in itself. Her hands lifted instinctively to scoop up her hair, piling it on top of her head to add another couple of inches to the height created by the sandals

'Wonderful!' Leonora applauded, confident enough of her own good looks to be generous. 'Silver and gold, with a hint of flame thrown in! You'll have every man present tonight foaming at the mouth!'

Nicole had to smile. 'Apart from Eduardo, of course.'

'Oh, Eduardo too. He's all man, I assure you.' She added with sincerity, 'I want the best there is for you, Nicole. If you married Patricio—'

'There's no chance of that,' Nicole interrupted firmly. 'His feelings apart, I don't have any for him.'

'It would be easy to develop some. He's a very good-looking young man.'

'It takes more than looks.' Nicole twisted to try and pull down the back zip, desisting when it caught in the material. 'Will you help me get out of this?'

'Only if you promise to wear it tonight,' came the answer. 'Otherwise you can struggle!'

'I'll ruin it if I pull the zip any further!'

Her stepmother shrugged. 'So ruin it. It cost the earth, but who cares?'

Gazing at her in frustration, Nicole gave in. 'All right, I'll wear the damn thing! Just get me out of it!'

Looking pleased with herself, Leonora obeyed, sliding the zip the whole way down and catching hold of the dress as Nicole stepped out of it. 'There,' she said, putting the garment back on its hanger. 'I'll come along later and help you into it again. Unless you'd prefer I sent someone else along?' she added with a wicked little glint. 'Marcos would prove a bigger challenge than Patricio, but he has a lot going for him.'

'I'd as soon tackle a grizzly bear,' Nicole countered, dousing the freshly struck spark with a dose of cold common sense. 'Knock it off, will you, Leo?'

The abbreviation drew a look of pain. 'You know how much I hate being called that!'

Nicole gave her a bland little smile. 'I'll do my best to remember. What time do guests start arriving?'

'We're expected to be ready and waiting by nine. Do you plan on resting until then?'

'Why not? I imagine it's going to be well into the early hours before we get to bed.'

Leonora sighed. 'As you like.'

Hopefully that was the last she would hear of this ridiculous campaign to get her married to one of the Peraza sons, thought Nicole wearily as the door closed behind her stepmother. It certainly wasn't what Marcos had in mind! Nor would she want it to be, for that matter. Men like him weren't husband material. Not by a long chalk!

She was ready all but the dress by eight-twenty. Wearing the satin wrap, she went outside to await Leonora's coming, relishing the night-time coolness.

The two long sides of the balcony were divided into individual portions by low, creeper-covered walls, providing a degree of privacy for the occupants of the rooms opening onto it, if only from the side view. Only two of the upper rooms on the opposite leg of the house were lit. One of them had the slatted shutters closed, while the other had both those and the outer glass doors flung wide to reveal part of the room within.

The man who came into view was naked except for the low-slung towel wrapped about his hips, shoulders gleaming in the soft glow from a lamp. Muscle ridged the midriff area; what back home would be called a fine six-pack, Nicole acknowledged, throat gone suddenly dry. The hair coating his upper chest was as thick and dark as that on his head; she could imagine the feel of it beneath her fingers.

As if sensing her regard, he looked towards the opened doors. It was too late to draw back. He had already seen her. Heart thudding, Nicole held his gaze, seeing his smile slowly widen. Only after a full twenty seconds had elapsed did she make a move, forcing herself to turn without haste and head back indoors.

She had herself in hand by the time Leonora arrived some minutes later. If Marcos thought she was going to be overcome by lust after seeing him in all his glory—or near enough—then he could think again, she told herself forcibly.

Leonora was wearing black, the strapless bodice revealing curves that owed nothing to artifice. Her skin was as smooth as Nicole's own, her upper arms just as firm and slender. They went down together to join the men in the salon. Expecting to see just Eduardo and Marcos, Nicole was caught off balance when Patricio leapt forward to seize her hand and raise it to his lips in unfeigned veneration.

'You are ravishing!' he exclaimed. '*Supremo!* You too, of course, Leonora,' he added, turning a glance on his stepmother-to-be. 'You will be the two most beautiful women here tonight!'

'Without doubt!' echoed his father happily. 'Come and sit with me, both of you, so that I may bask in your radiance for the moments remaining to us before our guests begin to arrive!'

'You look pretty magnificent yourself,' said Leonora

admiringly as he put his son aside to offer the two of them an arm each. 'You all do! Wouldn't you agree, Nicole?'

All three men were wearing the standard white tuxedo and dark trousers, with cummerbunds wrapping their waistlines—black for both Marcos and Eduardo, scarlet for Patricio. They looked, as Leonora had said, magnificent!

Nicole kept her tone light. *'Supremo!'*

'Thank you,' said Marcos on a dry note. 'You would like a drink while we wait?'

'A large one,' Leonora confirmed with a laugh. 'I need to settle my nerves before meeting all these people!'

'You have nothing to fear,' Eduardo assured her. 'They will all of them rejoice in my good fortune!'

Nicole concentrated her attention on Patricio, who was hovering close. 'I was under the impression you might be away for some time.'

'I found no great need for my continued presence,' he returned. 'I would have been desolated to be deprived of your beauty this evening!'

The flowery talk could possibly get on her nerves, thought Nicole, although Leonora appeared to lap it up. She contented herself with a smile by way of response, keeping it going as Marcos came over with the requested drinks.

'Gracias,' she said, taking the glass from him.

'You're welcome,' he returned smoothly. 'We'll be speaking your language the whole of this evening.'

For Leonora's sake; he didn't have to say it, the implication was obvious. Not that her stepmother appeared in any way concerned by her inability to communicate in the language of her new homeland, Nicole had to admit. She caught herself up on the verge of pointing out that it was actually an Americanism he had used, suspecting he was well aware of it. Sarcasm came all too easily to him.

Patricio had parked himself on the arm of the sofa—close enough for his sleeve to keep brushing her bare shoulder. He was acting as if he had some kind of priority claim on her, came the disquieting thought. She stole a swift glance at Marcos as he turned away, but there was nothing in his expression to indicate what he might be feeling.

She felt her insides turn liquid at the memory of how he had looked half an hour ago. The finest male body she had ever seen—which wasn't saying all that much, considering her limited experience, she supposed. Scott kept himself fit with regular sessions at the gym, but he was hardly in the same league. Not his fault, of course. Just a different body shape.

Her thoughts paused there in the sudden dismaying recollection that she still hadn't made the call home. It was too late again now. Not only would people be arriving any minute, but it was the early hours of the morning already in England.

Hopefully, she would have an opportunity to make the call when this affair finally ended, and catch Scott before he left for work. It wasn't going to be easy talking to him at all, knowing what she knew, but she could hardly tell him she was breaking things off over the phone.

The evening got under way with the arrival of a whole group of people together. Nicole soon gave up trying to tie names to faces; there were simply too many of them. After seeing the way these women dressed, she could only be glad that she had agreed to wear the silver gown. The green georgette would hardly have fitted the bill.

Leonora was proving a hit with everyone, it appeared—although perhaps just a little more with the men than the women. Eduardo rarely left her side, his hand clasping her waist in proud possession. To Nicole's growing irritation, Patricio was showing every sign of possessiveness himself. She longed to tell him to back off.

Ravishing in red, Isabella introduced her parents, a pleasant couple whom Nicole took to immediately. They were still chatting together when Marcos came up, accompanied by a young woman perhaps a year or two older than Isabella, though sufficiently like her to denote a relationship.

Sisters, it turned out, though their looks appeared to be the only point of resemblance. Elena had the confidence and poise of one accustomed to organising her own life. Her greeting was cool, lacking the congeniality displayed by her parents. Nicole had the distinct impression that to Elena her presence here in the Peraza household was not at all welcome. Tough! she thought, and saw from the look that sprang in the other girl's eyes that the message had got through.

If Marcos registered the sparks flying between the two of them, he gave no sign of it. He was, Nicole reflected, probably too well accustomed to provoking rivalry between his female acquaintances to pay it any heed.

The thought brought her up short. Rivalry be damned! In no way was she in competition for his attentions. No way!

CHAPTER FIVE

DINNER was served in the larger *comedor*, at a table that seemed to Nicole to stretch to infinity. The diamond earrings and bracelet that Leonora had also insisted on loaning her vied with a whole jeweller's store of gems in catching the light spilling from the huge silver candelabra set down in the centre of the table. A veritable royal banquet! she thought whimsically.

She had been seated with Patricio on one hand and Ramón Laniez on the other, while Marcos, almost directly opposite, had Elena and her mother. Some way down the long table Isabella was putting on a brave show, but it was apparent to anyone with any insight at all that her heart wasn't in it.

Nicole felt sorry for the girl. She was so thoroughly outclassed by her sister. If Marcos had any marital intentions at all, Elena would surely be the ideal choice for a man of his calibre.

As anticipated, the meal proved both long and filling. Nicole lost count of the courses. How people could eat such meals at this hour without being up half the night with galloping indigestion she found hard to credit. Even the comparatively small amount she had actually eaten herself was proving more than enough by the time coffee was served.

A move back to the *salón* around one o'clock brought some relief. Nicole took advantage of a time when Patricio's attention was turned elsewhere to slip outside for a breath of fresh air. There was more seating further down the covered terrace, outside the range of the light spilling from the *salón*. Just a few minutes, she promised herself, then back to the fray!

The sky was clear, the stars so much bigger and brighter than they ever looked back home. Sitting there, she felt a sense of isolation. She didn't belong here; could never belong here. She was out of her depth in every sense.

Considering that she was only here for a limited period anyway, it hardly mattered. By this time next week she would be back in familiar surroundings among people of her own kind. Starting a new life too. Much as she hated the idea of hurting Scott, it had to be done, for both their sakes. He wouldn't go short of feminine companionship anyway. There were several who'd be more than happy to step into her shoes.

Someone opened the door through which she had emerged a few minutes ago, emitting a brief burst of sound. Nicole found herself holding her breath as the light revealed the identity of the newcomer, half-hoping, half-fearing that he was looking for her.

Marcos closed the door again and stood for a moment viewing the immediate vicinity before widening his sights. Seated as she was in deep shadow, Nicole thought he might not see her, but the silver dress was a give-away, reflecting the moonlight as she incautiously moved a leg.

'Why are you hiding yourself away out here?' he asked, moving towards her. 'Do our friends intimidate you?'

'Of course not,' she denied. 'I just needed to be on my own for a moment or two, that's all.'

'Why?'

She gave a brief shrug. 'I'm usually in bed by this hour.'

'There is nothing to stop you from going there this moment if you wish it.' Marcos had come to a halt a bare yard away, hands resting lightly on the back of the adjoining chair, his expression obscured by the shadows.

'That would be unforgivably rude of me,' she said.

'A little impolite, perhaps, but not unforgivably so. People are unlikely to begin leaving before two o'clock. Do you see yourself lasting until then?'

'If it kills me!' she declared, opting to make a joke of it. 'Never let it be said that the British lack stamina!'

'A few minutes more will do no harm,' he said as she started to rise. 'I find the night air pleasant myself.'

Nicole subsided again, her heart beating a light fandango against her ribs as he moved around the chair to take a seat on the long padded bench at her side. He was close enough for her to feel his body heat—to catch the emotive scent of aftershave or cologne. The faint beading of perspiration along her upper lip owed nothing to air temperature; neither did the shiver that coursed the length of her spine as his sleeve brushed her arm.

'Everyone will be wondering where you are,' she said a little desperately, wanting him to go and to stay at one and the same time. 'Especially Elena.'

'Elena will suffer no loneliness,' he said. 'Relax, *querida*.'

The word meant nothing, Nicole told herself, unable to follow the injunction with every nerve doing exactly the opposite. She was a long, long way from being this man's darling! His fancy, perhaps. No, not even perhaps. He wanted her. He had made that clear enough this morning. But that was all he wanted from her.

'Why did you follow me out here?' she asked, deciding to take the bull by the horns, in a manner of speaking.

He lifted a brow. 'Must there be a reason?'

'With you, there would always be a reason,' she said flatly. 'If you were hoping to find me in receptive mood for your overtures, you can think again!'

'The thought of making love to you may have occurred to me,' he admitted imperturbably. 'As it no doubt occurred to every man present on seeing you tonight. You have a beautiful body. The dress merely serves to outline it for the eye to fully appreciate. If you dislike the idea of being desired, you should have worn something less likely to arouse such an emotion.'

'I didn't have anything of my own that was suitable for the occasion,' Nicole claimed. 'This belongs to Leonora.'

'Really?' Marcos sounded surprised. 'She must be remarkably lacking in feminine jealousy.'

Nicole made an impatient gesture. 'She's no cause to be jealous of anyone, much less me! If you tried getting to know her a little better, you'd realise how generous a person she can be.'

'My only concern is that she continues to make my father happy,' came the unmoved response. 'I have no desire to form a closer relationship with her myself.' He paused, dark eyes glinting as he studied her upturned face. 'You, now, are a different matter.'

Nicole stiffened as the arm laid along the bench-back slid about her shoulders, but the urge to just go with the flow was too strong for her. She closed her eyes as he put his lips to the pulse beating so wildly at her temple. The kisses he laid down the line of her cheek were featherlight, yet left a trail of fire on her skin.

She was trembling in every limb by the time he reached her mouth, the afternoon's vows forgotten. She opened her lips to him, tasting him the way he was tasting her, clinging to him, arms about his neck, breasts pressed against the hardness of his chest. She wanted to be closer still, to be free of the intruding clothing. Scott, home, the future beyond this moment were of no consequence.

The sense of deprivation when he put her from him again was almost too much for her.

'Enough for now,' he said softly. 'I must return to our guests. You feel able to accompany me?'

Nicole found her voice with an effort. 'What will people think if we go back indoors together?'

'They may think what they will.' Marcos was already on his feet, holding out a hand to assist her to hers. 'Come, *mi amor*.'

Meant or not, the endearment warmed her. She took the proffered hand, allowing him to draw her upright. He slid an arm about her waist as they moved towards the *salón*—a gesture she would have found annoyingly over-possessive had it come from Patricio.

The difference being that she would welcome being possessed by Marcos, came the treacherous thought. In every sense of the word!

As anticipated, their return to the salon together by no means went unnoticed, although neither of the Laniez girls were in the immediate vicinity, Nicole was glad to note.

If a definite arrangement existed between Marcos and Elena, he would surely avoid giving rise to the kind of speculation she saw in several pairs of eyes, she told herself, doing her best to act naturally. Elena might appear on the face of it to be the perfect wife for him, but it didn't necessarily mean that *he* saw it that way.

Whether or not, she'd be a fool to let things go any further than they already had, she told herself forcibly. She wasn't equipped to walk away unscathed from the kind of relationship she was sure was all Marcos had in mind.

It was indeed around two o'clock before people began leaving; almost three when the last finally departed. Nicole weathered a glowering look from Isabella when the Laniez family took their leave, followed by another, even more vitriolic one, from her sister. Gossip, she gathered, travelled no less fast here than back home.

'A very successful evening,' declared Eduardo with satisfaction, loosening his tie. He lifted Leonora's hand to his lips. 'You were everything I could have asked of you, *amada*! You also, *niña*,' he added to Nicole. 'We are privileged indeed to have two such beautiful additions to our family.'

'Yes indeed!' agreed Patricio. 'You must come and spend your life here with us!'

'Nicole has a life of her own back in England,' said Marcos levelly. 'Why should she want to leave it?'

'Because she is a part of us now,' declared his brother. 'An addition to our family, as Father says.'

'Marcos is right,' Nicole broke in before he could answer. 'Much as I appreciate the sentiment, I do have a life back home. One I couldn't contemplate giving up.'

'Then we must be satisfied to have you visit us regularly instead,' said Eduardo. 'You will do that?'

'Of course.' Nicole forbore from pointing out that her job alone would limit the regularity. She gave him her warmest smile. 'I really am grateful for all your kindness.'

Silent up until now, Leonora let out a resigned sigh. 'There are times,' she observed, 'when I wonder why I bother!' She shook her head as Nicole made to speak. 'There's nothing more to say. I'm sure we're all ready to retire for the night—or what's left of it.'

'But of course.' Eduardo was all solicitousness. 'You are not yet fully accustomed to our practices.' He took her arm, his very touch reverent. 'We will say good-night. There is, of course, no reason for you to rise early,' he added to Nicole.

More than could be said for the servants still clearing away, she reflected as the two departed. It would be gone seven already back home. If she was going to telephone Scott at all, it had to be within the next half an hour. There was no extension in her room, which made things even more difficult.

She didn't really want to make the call at all, she acknowledged ruefully, but there was no way round it. Left without contact any longer, Scott was likely to call here. Marcos had had a low enough opinion of her to start with. She hated to think what his reaction would be on discovering that she had a fiancé back home.

She came back to earth with a start as Patricio said her name, to find both brothers looking at her with odd expressions.

'I'm sorry,' she said, 'I was…drifting.'

'Time, as Leonora said, that we all retired,' Patricio declared. 'I shall see you to your room.'

'I'm sure Nicole is more than capable of finding her way there alone.' Marcos indicated the door leading out to the hall. 'If you're ready.'

It was unlikely at this hour that he had any intention

of attempting to continue what they had begun outside, Nicole reassured herself. It was even possible that his interest in her had waned over the past hour or two.

She was kidding herself, of course. He wasn't about to pass up on what must appear to be pretty much a dead cert! It was going to be up to her to say no and mean it when the time came.

Patricio stuck close by her side until they reached the parting of the ways at the top of the stairs, taking his leave with open reluctance to accompany his brother across to the other wing of the house.

Hoping the staff would also have retired by the time she finished undressing, Nicole got out of her finery and donned the long smooth nightdress that went with the satin wrap, sliding her feet into cream brocade mules. The whole house was silent when she cautiously opened her door again. Eduardo and Leonora's suite was on this side of the courtyard, but further along, so they were unlikely to hear her going downstairs.

She was thankful for the low lights left burning. Making her way back downstairs in darkness would have been hazardous. There was a telephone in the hall, but it would be safer to make the call from the *salón*, she decided. She needed to hurry if she was to catch Scott before he left the flat.

The first time she forgot to leave the 0 out of the area code, and had to dial again. Even then she still had to go through the operator. The ringing tone seemed to go on for ever. She was about to give up when the receiver was finally lifted.

Scott barely waited for the operator to finish her announcement. 'Nicole, what the devil happened?' he demanded. 'I was stuck here like a dummy all last night waiting for you to call!'

His gym night, Nicole remembered belatedly. He would have hated missing that. 'I'm really sorry,' she said. 'This is the first chance I've had to get to a phone at the right time.'

The mention of time gave him pause for a moment. 'It must be around half past three in the morning there!' he said. 'What on earth—'

'There was a party. I had to wait until everyone had gone. I'm fine,' she added swiftly. 'How are you?'

'Okay now I've heard from you.' He was calming down a little. 'If you hadn't rung by tonight I was going to ring that number you left me.'

Nicole drew in a breath and let it out again slowly. 'Well, you don't need to now. Things are pretty hectic, with all the wedding preparations and everything, so I'll probably not be around if you do ring.'

'I see.' There was another pause, a change of tone. 'How are things?'

'Very good. Eduardo is everything Leonora claimed him to be.'

'And the sons?'

'They're fine too. I'll have to go,' she said, unable to stall any further. 'I'm nearly falling asleep on my feet! Take care of yourself.'

She replaced the receiver before he could make any answer, standing there with her hand resting on it feeling a total heel. There was a limit to dissimulation. It might even have been fairer to tell him the truth.

'Who were you calling at this hour?' asked Marcos from the open doorway.

It took Nicole a moment or two to find her voice. Wearing a black silk robe, feet thrust into leather mules, he was no less of a force to be reckoned with.

'I only just remembered I hadn't let anyone know

I'd arrived safely,' she said, striving to keep her tone easy. 'I thought I'd catch them before they left for work.'

'You had no problem getting through?'

She shook her head, beginning to recover her wits. 'None at all. The operator was very efficient.'

'It would help that you speak the language.' He paused, eyes too perceptive by half. 'Your friend was no doubt relieved to hear your voice.'

'Very.' Nicole tried to recall just what she had said, wondering how long he had been standing there. She hadn't actually used Scott's name; that much she did know. In fact she was pretty sure there had been nothing in the conversation to indicate the sex of the other party at all.'

'What brought you down again, anyway?' she asked. 'I didn't think I'd made any noise.'

'You made no noise,' he confirmed. 'When I found your room empty I took the logical course in assuming that you must have come back downstairs for some reason.'

Green eyes darkened as the initial part of the statement struck home. 'I suppose I don't need ask *why* you went to my room?' she said. 'You expected me to be ready and waiting for you!'

'I take nothing for granted,' he returned equably. 'Even when the invitation is clear.'

Nicole stuck both hands in the side pockets of her wrap, nails digging into her palms. There was only one way to go, and that was to play the bitch. He wouldn't like it, but it would get her off the hook she had forged for herself.

'A couple of kisses hardly constitute an invitation,'

she scorned. 'Not where I come from, anyway. I don't have the least intention of sleeping with you!'

'I had no intention of sleeping with *you*,' he said after a moment, the silky softness of his voice more telling of his mood than any invective. The dark eyes skimmed the length of her body, expression infinitely disturbing. 'We both of us knew from the beginning what was to happen between us.'

'"The beginning", in case you've forgotten, was scarcely more than twenty-four hours ago!' Nicole clipped. 'And we knew nothing of the kind! You treated me like a pariah!'

'I was fighting my instincts.' Marcos hadn't moved from the room entrance, yet suddenly seemed to loom closer—dangerously closer. 'I saw a beautiful flame-haired English girl and I wanted her. As I want her still. Time has no bearing.'

Nicole could feel her heart hammering into her throat, the growing dampness between her thighs. She wanted him too; there was no denying it. The very thought of going back upstairs with him, of surrendering herself into those strong arms and making passionate, abandoned love throughout what remained of the night...

'I'm sorry if I led you to believe I was of the same mind,' she said huskily, forgetting the bitchy role. 'I—'

'You're saying you have no desire for me?' The dark eyes took on a gleam visible even from where she stood. 'Then prove it to me.'

Nicole made an attempt to evade him as he came swiftly over, but he foiled her, one hand snaking about her waist to draw her to him, the other clasping the back of her neck to hold her head still as he claimed her lips. Had the kiss been savage, she could have fought it, but his mouth was unexpectedly gentle, almost teasing, melting her resistance like ice under a hot sun.

He was naked beneath the robe; she could tell that instantly. Without conscious volition, she ran her fingers inside the rolled collar to feel the springy softness of his chest hair, murmuring incoherent words against his lips. She had never known anything like the sensations flooding her, heat spreading from the pit of her stomach to engulf every part of her body, inner thighs spasming as he cupped her buttocks to draw her closer still, sore muscles forgotten. She felt his hardness, his readiness pressuring her thighs apart; she wanted to sink to the floor and draw him down on top of her, to have him fill her with that throbbing shaft and appease the gnawing hunger.

All thoughts of resistance had faded to a place where they no longer held any impact. She relished his strength when he swung her up into his arms to carry her from the *salón* and up the stairs, pressing her face into his neck to kiss the warm skin, the very scent of him increasing the tumult inside her. Nothing else mattered right now but this man, this feeling.

Her door was standing open, the bedside lamps casting a soft glow. Marcos set her down slowly, allowing his hands to glide over her body as if to register every line. His eyes were dark pools lit by tiny flickering flames; Nicole felt herself drowning in their depths. She touched a finger to the sensual curve of his lips, tremoring as he drew the tip of it into his mouth.

She made no move to stop him when he eased open the belt of her wrap and pushed the garment back over her shoulders to fall with satin smoothness and silence to the floor. Her nightdress had narrow shoulder straps.

He eased those down her arms, drawing a roughened breath as the material slid free of her breasts. Cut to outline the figure, the garment stuck at waist level, needing a helping hand to smooth it over her hips so that it could slide the rest of the way down the length of her legs.

Marcos held her away from him to view her in her entirety, the expression that came over his face roughening her own breath. Reaching out a hand, she undid the belt of his robe to allow the material to fall open. As anticipated, he was naked beneath—and already fully aroused. Nicole used the same fingertips to trace the ridges of muscle, feeling him quiver. His hipbone was flat, with no surplus flesh to pad it. He made a guttural sound deep in his throat as she enclosed him, drawing her back to him to kiss her with an almost savage intensity before swinging her once more in his arms to carry her to the bed.

The mattress felt firm to her back. Marcos stood for a moment to strip off the robe, then he came down to her, stretching his body alongside her and propping himself on an elbow to allow the run of his free hand over the curve of her hip and waist to reach her uptilted breast. Nicole watched his face as he explored the full shape, catching her breath when he lowered his head to take her peaking, aching nipple between his lips. His tongue was a flickering flame against the tender skin—an agony she could scarcely bear yet didn't want to stop. Her whole body craved for his touch.

As if in response to that desire, he slid the back of his fingers very, very slowly and softly down between her breasts and over her fluttering stomach muscles, lingering for an endless moment at the very edge of the downy cluster before moving again to glide between her trembling thighs.

'*Flor de mi corazón!*' he breathed as he penetrated her secret depths.

Flower of my heart! The small part of Nicole's mind still functioning on a rational level knew that they were just words, but it made no difference to her responses. She had entered a world where sensation took precedence over rationality, where all she cared about was having it continue!

She opened to him eagerly, urgently when he finally brought his weight to bear, wrapping her legs about him as he slid all the way inside her. It felt so wonderfully right to be together this way—as if he was made for her and she for him alone. She wanted to stay like this for all time, holding him, encompassing him—content just to have him a part of her.

A contentment that faded the moment he began to move, giving way to a mounting frenzy of emotion as the pace gathered, until nothing else existed but that driving force.

Recovery from the mind-shattering climax was by no means immediate for either of them. Nicole felt she might never find the energy to move a muscle again. This was the way it should be, she thought mistily. *This* was what was missing from her life!

Marcos was the first to stir, lifting his head to look into her drowned face with eyes still holding the memory of those tumultuous moments.

'I anticipated a great deal from you,' he said softly, 'but you outclassed my expectations. A woman of fire all the way through!' He bent to press a delicate kiss to each eye, following it with an even more delicate touch of his lips to the end of her nose. 'Once will not be enough. Already I feel myself reviving!'

Nicole could feel it too. Neither was she loath to repeat the experience. What she couldn't stop from creeping in was the guilt. Her decision to break things off with Scott was no excuse for rushing into bed with a man she hadn't even met two days ago. What that made her she hated to consider.

'This should never have happened,' she whispered painfully. 'I didn't mean it to happen!'

Marcos gave a slow smile. 'Yes, you did. But, like so many women, you felt it necessary to deny your nature.'

'I didn't say I didn't *want* it to happen,' she got out. 'Only that it shouldn't have happened.'

'Why not?' He sounded perplexed. 'We are two adult people with the same needs. Why should we not indulge them?'

Drawing in a shallow breath, she said thickly, 'For one thing, because I've probably given you the impression that I do this kind of thing all the time.'

'If I believed that I would not be here with you,' he declared.

Nicole searched the olive-skinned features, not at all sure what it was she was looking for. 'But you obviously realise I'm not a virgin.'

The strong mouth creased. 'You most certainly are not now!'

'You know what I mean.' It was getting more and more difficult to find the words. 'You weren't the first man to make love to me.'

'That much I *had* gathered,' he said drily.

'It...doesn't matter to you?'

The smile came again. 'We live in an enlightened

age, *querida*. No virgin could have given me the pleasure you provided just now.' He stirred his lower body, eyes firing afresh as he watched her face constrict. 'And I mean to claim it once more,' he added softly.

Nicole opened her eyes to early-morning sunlight, unsurprised to find herself alone. Marcos was hardly going to risk being seen leaving her room.

The guilt returned full strength as mind and body recalled the night's licentiousness. While Marcos might consider her entitled in this enlightened age to exercise a certain freedom of choice, he'd ten to one hold a very different view if he discovered she was in a supposedly committed relationship.

Hardly likely that he would find out in the few days remaining of her stay, came the bleak thought. This time next week it would all be over. She'd be a fool, she knew, to allow herself any further involvement with him if she wanted to leave here with her deeper emotions intact, but she doubted her ability to resist if faced with the same temptation. Which she would be; he'd already made that much clear.

Enjoy today, worry about tomorrow when it came, she told herself in sudden reckless resolve. Whatever happened, she'd handle it.

CHAPTER SIX

SHE WAS disappointed to be greeted by Patricio alone when she went down to breakfast, wondering where Marcos was. He didn't seem the type to sleep in, no matter how strenuous a night he'd spent.

'Today we drive to Caracas!' the former declared.

'I don't really feel up to it,' Nicole said hastily. 'Not after such a late night.' She was horrified to feel herself colouring as the images intruded, hoping he wouldn't notice.

He looked disappointed himself, but was obviously ready to fall in with her wishes. 'Perhaps tomorrow then?'

She would prefer not to go at all, only she could hardly say so. 'That would be nice,' she agreed. 'I'll look forward to it.'

'No more than I shall myself,' he assured her. 'It will be a day to remember for both of us!'

If there was one characteristic the brothers shared, it was self-confidence, Nicole reflected, summoning a weak smile. Marcos had shown it in abundance last night. All she had shown was a total lack of moral fibre. The easiest conquest he'd probably ever made!

'Are you feeling ill?' asked Patricio on a note of concern.

'A little too much wine last night,' she said with a suitably wry expression, her earlier resolve already beginning to wilt. 'Nothing that won't pass.'

'I have suffered from the malady myself on occasion,' he advised with sympathy. 'You should eat something.'

Food would choke her, she thought leadenly. She was on the verge of using the spurious nausea as an excuse to make her escape when Eduardo put in an appearance. He was alone, though looking no less content with life.

'You show more stamina than your stepmama,' he remarked with humour. 'I was invited to vanish in the most inelegant of phrases when I suggested waiting while she finished dressing. I decided it was perhaps best that she have breakfast served in the bedroom.'

'The morning after the night before, as my father used to say!' Nicole could have sunk through the floor the moment the words left her lips. 'I'm sorry,' she said uncomfortably. 'He's the last person you'll want reminding of.'

'Why should I feel animosity towards your father?' asked Eduardo in obviously genuine surprise. 'From what Leonora tells me, he was a good man for whom she had the deepest regard.'

'You don't mind, then,' she said after a moment, 'that she...loved someone else before you?'

If Eduardo had noted the slight hesitation before the word 'loved', he gave no sign of it, his smile untroubled. 'No two loves are ever the same, niña.' He turned his attention to Patricio. 'You appear unexpectedly alert yourself his morning.'

'I had thoughts of taking Nicole to Caracas,' his son acknowledged ruefully, 'but she feels herself indisposed.'

'Nothing serious,' Nicole claimed hurriedly as Eduardo turned her a concerned glance. 'There's still plenty of time before the wedding.'

'You intend leaving us as soon as the wedding is over?' he asked.

'Well, the following day, at any rate,' she said, smothering the despondency induced by the mere thought. 'You and Leonora will be heading off somewhere on your own, I imagine.'

'True,' he agreed with a smile. 'I have promised her a *luna de miel* to remember. But my sons will still be here,' he added. 'They will both of them be reluctant to lose your company so soon.'

'That's right!' Patricio confirmed. 'You've come too far to spend only these few days with us.'

A great deal further than he knew, she thought with a pang. Aloud, she said levelly, 'I have a job to get back to, I'm afraid.'

'If you came here to live, as family, you would have no need to work,' said Eduardo, either forgetting or deliberately ignoring the previous evening's conversation.

Nicole could imagine Marcos's reaction should she take up that invitation. If she'd had any inclination at all, the situation now would have made it impossible.

'Will you at least consider it?' he urged when she made no immediate reply.

It was simpler, she decided, to agree than to issue a flat refusal. 'All right,' she said, 'I'll consider it. And thank you for the thought.'

From the expression in his eyes, he was far from deceived, but he made no further reference. 'It isn't like Marcos to lie abed,' he remarked instead, glancing at the slim gold watch on his wrist.

'I believe he agreed to ride with Elena this morning,' advised Patricio.

'It's time he made his intentions towards her clear,'

declared his father. 'Our ways may be different from what they were in the past, but there are still certain rules of conduct to be followed. I find it surprising that Ramón shows so little concern for his daughter's future.'

Patricio gave a brief laugh. 'Not so much a lack of concern, perhaps, as the realisation that his word bears little weight with her. I've no doubt she'd marry Marcos tomorrow if he asked her. But then, so would Isabella. A good thing I have other interests, or I might be jealous,' he added to Nicole on a flippant note that somehow rang a little hollow.

She made some suitably flattering response, unable to stifle the pangs of jealousy herself at the thought of the two of them out there in the woods together. Not that it made any difference whether Marcos intended marrying Elena or not. She was under no illusions as to *her* place in his scheme of things.

She was resting on a lounger—having managed to convince Patricio that she was better left alone to recover from her malady—when Marcos finally put in an appearance. He came as he had done the day before to perch on the edge, bending to kiss her with a liberty that grated. She kept her lips firmly closed, her senses under strict control.

He wasted neither time nor effort on persuasion, raising his head to view her with drawn brows. 'Why?' was all he said.

Nicole hardened heart and mind against the desire to give way, keeping a steady regard by sheer effort of will. 'One swallow doesn't make a summer.'

The dark brows drew even further together. 'If by that you mean you have no further desire for me, I refuse to believe it!'

'It isn't the lack of desire,' she said, 'just a refusal to be taken for granted. Last night was good'—that had to be understatement of the year—'but it doesn't mean I'm going to be available for the asking.'

'You expect me to beg!'

Nicole managed a dry little smile. 'I expect you to back off when I tell you to. I realise, of course, that you're unaccustomed to being turned down, but there has to be a first time for everything.'

The firm mouth was a thin, tight line, the expression in his eyes daunting. 'You will find,' he said softly, 'that our ways with women who play such games are very much different from those of your countrymen.'

'I told you before, it's no game!' she denied, finding strength in an anger of her own. 'I made a mistake I'm not about to repeat, that's all. If you can't accept it, you can...do the other thing!'

For a lengthy moment the fury continued to blaze in the dark eyes, then unexpectedly it faded, taken over by a startling glimmer of humour. 'What exactly is this "other thing" you wish me to do?'

Thrown completely off balance, Nicole gazed at him in confounded silence. The last thing she had expected from him was amusement!

'I'm not joking,' she got out.

'That much I realise,' he returned. 'Which leaves me to draw but one conclusion. Your pride is at stake because you believe my interest in you is no more than I might have in a streetwalker—should I ever find myself in quite such desperate straits.' He put out a hand to stroke her cheek, mouth stretching into a smile when she failed to repulse the gesture. 'You do yourself an injustice. No man could regard you in such a sense. You are a beautiful, passionate woman of the world!'

A woman of the world she most certainly was not, she wanted to tell him, but the words stuck in her throat. In his book, any woman who allowed a man the kind of intimacies they had shared outside of marriage could be nothing else.

Unlikely, in which case, that he would be taking prior advantage of Elena's attractions, came the thought—for what comfort there was in it.

'You still wish me to…back off?' he asked.

The sensible answer would be yes, only she found herself incapable of saying that too—just as she had known she would be.

'I was being over-sensitive,' she said instead, abandoning the struggle. 'Forget I spoke, will you?'

'That would be difficult,' he returned with mock seriousness. 'You have a wicked tongue. The next time you lash me with it I may retaliate in kind, so be warned!'

'I'll keep a check on it,' she promised.

Giving a free rein to recklessness, she lifted both hands to cup his face and draw him down to her, putting her lips to his in unbridled demand. His response was immediate, hand seeking her breast, fingers cupping her shape in total familiarity.

It was Nicole who had begun it, and she who reluctantly ended it as the memory of where they were finally broke through.

'Someone might come!' she exclaimed, pressing him away again.

'Someone might indeed,' he agreed regretfully. 'We must wait for a more conducive time. Tonight,' he added with a gleam, 'our hours together will be longer.'

If she was going to do this at all, she might as well go the whole hog, Nicole concluded. Four more days, including the wedding day. Five whole nights! There was every possibility that she was going to finish up losing far more than her basic integrity, but that was a risk she would just have to take.

'I must go now and change my clothing,' he said, getting to his feet. 'Then we'll take a drive, the two of us.'

It hadn't struck Nicole up until that moment that he was still wearing riding gear. He must have come to her straight from Elena. So what? she thought doggedly. Whatever his long-term plans where the other was concerned, there was no definite commitment as yet; Patricio had confirmed that much.

Patricio! She came jerkily upright. 'I can't go with you! I told your brother I was suffering from a hangover.'

Marcos lifted broad shoulders. 'So? You recovered.'

'You don't understand. He wanted to take me to Caracas.'

'If you didn't wish to go, you only had to tell him so,' came the matter-of-fact comment. 'Why lie about it?'

'I didn't want to hurt his feelings,' she admitted.

Marcos studied her for a moment, expression difficult to decipher. 'You believe his emotions reliant on your indulgence?'

'No, of course not. I only meant—' She broke off, eyed him indeterminately, said slowly, 'Was there really a need for him to go to Guayana, or was it just a ploy to save him from my clutches?'

'More of the latter than the former.' The acknowledgement was made without any sign of discomfiture. 'You were showing a great deal too much interest in him.'

MILLS & BOON ®

An Important Message from The Editors of Mills & Boon®

Dear Reader,

Because you've chosen to read one of our romance novels, we'd like to say "thank you"!

And, as a **special way** to thank you, we've selected <u>four more</u> of the <u>books</u> you love so much **and** a welcome gift to send you absolutely <u>FREE!</u>

Please enjoy them with our compliments...

Tessa Shapcott

Editor, Mills & Boon

P.S. And because we value our customers we've attached something extra inside...

PEEL OFF AND PLACE INSIDE

How to validate your Editor's Free Gift "Thank You"

1. **Peel off the Free Gift Seal** from the front cover. Place it in the space provided to the right. This automatically entitles you to receive four free books and a beautiful goldtone Austrian crystal necklace.

2. **Complete your details** on the card, detach along the dotted line, and post it back to us. No stamp needed. We'll then send you four free novels from the Presents...™ series. These books have a retail value of £2.40, but are yours to keep absolutely free.

3. **Enjoy the read.** We hope that after receiving your free books you'll want to remain a subscriber. But the choice is yours - to continue or cancel, any time at all! So why not accept our no risk invitation? You'll be glad you did.

Your satisfaction is guaranteed

You're under no obligation to buy anything. We charge you nothing for your introductory parcel. And you don't have to make any minimum number of purchases – not even one! Thousands of readers have already discovered that the Reader Service is the most convenient way of enjoying the latest new romance novels before they are available in the shops. Of course, postage and packing is completely FREE.

Tessa Shapcott
Editor, Mills & Boon

◀ **Detach and keep your complimentary book mark**

The Editor's "Thank You"

You'll love this exquisite gold-plated necklace with its 18" cobra linked chain and multi-faceted Austrian crystal which sparkles just like a diamond. It's the perfect accessory to dress up any outfit, casual or formal. RESPOND TODAY AND IT'S YOURS FREE.

Not actual size

Yes! Please send me my four FREE books and a welcome gift

PLACE EDITOR'S "THANK YOU" SEAL HERE

Yes! I have placed my free gift seal in the space provided above. Please send me my four free books along with my welcome gift. I understand I am under no obligation to purchase any books, as explained on the back and opposite page. I am over 18 years of age.

POFI

Surname (Mrs/Ms/Miss/Mr) _____Initials_____

Address_____

_____

_____

_____Postcode _____

▶ **Detach along the dotted line and post this card today. No Stamp Needed ▶**

HOW THE READER SERVICE WORKS

Accepting the free books places you under no obligation to buy anything. You may keep the books and gift and return the despatch note marked "cancel". If we don't hear from you, about a month later we will send you 6 brand new books and invoice you for only £2.40* each. That's the complete price – there is no extra charge for postage and packing. You may cancel at any time, otherwise every month we'll send you 6 more books, which you may either purchase or return – the choice is yours.

*Terms and prices subject to change without notice.

The Reader Service™
FREEPOST CN81
CROYDON
CR9 3WZ

NO
STAMP
NEEDED

If this offer card is missing, please write to: The Reader Service, P.O. Box 236, Croydon, CR9 3RU

'Oh, come on! He was hardly going to go overboard for someone he'd only just met!'

'On the contrary. He was captivated the moment he set eyes on you. It seemed a good policy to get him out of your way for a time, before he lost his head completely.'

Green eyes flared. 'You believed I was out to secure myself a husband at any price!'

'At the time, perhaps. I didn't know you then.'

'You don't know me now,' she said, shaking her head impatiently as he lifted a meaningful eyebrow. 'The *real* me. All you're interested in is my body.'

'If that was so,' he returned, 'I could gain the same pleasure from any well-formed woman. There is far more to you than your shape, tempting though it is. I look forward to exploring your inner self.'

'There's hardly going to be time for any in-depth analysis either way,' Nicole pointed out. 'I'll be leaving the day after the wedding.'

The pause seemed to stretch to infinity, although it was no more than a few seconds in reality. As always, there was no reading the mind behind the dark eyes, no telling anything at all from his expression.

'As you say,' he agreed, 'time is pressing. So we must use every moment, must we not?'

So what had she expected? Nicole asked herself as he went indoors. That he would insist she stayed longer? Unlike his father, he had no long-term interest in her. Out of sight, she would be out of mind within minutes.

She got up and went to sit on the low stone wall surrounding the central fountain, dabbling her fingers in the water. The sun felt so good after weeks of indifferent weather back home. At this altitude the heat would never become overpowering even in high summer. If she accepted Eduardo's invitation she would never have to face an English winter again.

Marcos aside, doing what exactly? came the thought. She hardly saw herself living the idle life. There would be the question of money, for one thing. She had little of her own, and in no way could she accept being totally financed. No, it was just a pipedream. An idea Eduardo himself probably hadn't thought all the way through.

'You're a regular dark horse!' said Leonora at her back, making her start. 'All that guff about staying faithful to Scott, and you've got *both* of them jumping though hoops!'

Nicole turned to look at her stepmother, doing her best to keep her face from reflecting her inner turbulence. 'What are you talking about?'

Leonora laughed. 'Come off it! I saw you with Marcos just now. If the two of you didn't spend last night together, I'd say you were definitely on line for tonight. Of the two of them, I still think you'd stand a better chance with Patricio, but I have to admit that Marcos has the edge when it comes to sheer pulling power!'

'Stop it!' Nicole took refuge in anger. 'I don't know what you think you saw—'

'I'm a long way from blind,' the older woman interrupted drily. 'The way he was touching you, it certainly wasn't the first time. A bit risky in broad daylight, if you didn't want to be seen—although men do tend to be pretty one-track in that direction.

'I'm not condemning you, darling,' she continued, softening her tone. 'Far from it. The only reservation I have is regarding your chances of getting Marcos to the point of proposing. You'd have stood a far better chance with Patricio.'

Nicole got to her feet, steeling herself against the strong desire to just walk away. This had to be sorted out once and for all.

'Whatever the situation between Marcos and me, there's no question of my marrying him, or even wanting to,' she said. 'I'm going home after the wedding.'

'To Scott?'

If she said no it would only cause further complications, Nicole decided swiftly. 'Why not?' she asked.

Leonora eyed her in silence for a moment, as if attempting to weigh her up. 'Just a fling, then?' she said at length. 'I didn't think you were the type.'

The shrug was designed to signify nonchalance. 'We're all entitled to a little fun before we settle down.'

'Scott included?'

'Why not?' Nicole said again. 'For all I know, he's having a high old time himself while I'm away.'

'And pigs might fly!' Leonora shook her head. 'Still, if you're happy to settle for a brief affair, who am I to complain? At the very least it seems to have taken Marcos's mind off other matters for the time being.'

Smarting, Nicole was sorely tempted to leave her to stew, but her basic nature got the better of her. 'He's decided to give you a chance to prove yourself,' she said. 'So long as you treat his father the right way, he'll stay out of it.'

'Well, hallelujah!' The blue eyes held a derisive glint. 'I don't know how I'd have coped without you.'

'I doubt if you'd find *him* easy to cope with if you did let Eduardo down,' Nicole warned, paying the sarcasm no heed.

Derision gave way to sobriety. 'I've no intention of

it. So far as I'm concerned, this marriage is to death! Of course,' she added on a practical note, 'he's likely to be the one to go first. Let's hope I'll still look good in black by then.'

Nicole had to laugh. 'You're incorrigible!' she exclaimed.

'I know.' Leonora was smiling again too. 'I mean it, though. I've far too much regard for Eduardo to even consider anyone else.'

'I'm glad.' Nicole stirred herself. 'I'd better go and tidy up. Marcos is taking me for a drive.' She held up a staying hand as her stepmother opened her mouth to speak. 'Not another word!'

'I was just going to say have a nice day,' came the innocent return. 'Or morning, at any rate—what's left of it. What shall I tell Patricio if he asks where you are?'

'The truth. What else?' Nicole was already moving away, unable to take any more. Just a fling, Leonora had called it. To all intents and purposes, that was right. What she couldn't do was allow it to matter.

If the limousine in which Marcos had picked her up from the airport had taken her breath away, the long red Ferrari certainly shortened it. Sliding into the low-slung passenger seat, Nicole was thankful that she had had the foresight to change into tailored trousers and shirt. The dress she had been wearing would have left little to the imagination.

Not that she'd have been showing anything he wasn't already intimately acquainted with, she had to admit.

'Where are we going?' she asked as he headed the car down the long winding driveway. 'I mean, it's only a couple of hours till lunch.'

'If you're hungry already we can call somewhere,' he said.

'I'm not hungry. I just wondered if you intended coming back for lunch, that's all.'

'It will depend,' he returned equably, 'on how far we go. Perhaps we may even reach Caracas.'

'That would be like kicking Patricio in the teeth,' she protested. 'I already told you he plans on taking me there himself tomorrow.'

'You will be going nowhere with my brother,' was the unequivocal reply.

Green eyes sparked. 'Is that a fact!'

'That,' he confirmed, 'is a fact.' He glanced her way. 'You'd prefer to be with Patricio this moment?'

Nicole let out an exasperated breath. 'You can take this dominant male thing too far.'

'With a woman such as yourself, there is no "too far",' he declared. 'And you didn't answer the question.'

'You know the answer,' she said. 'If I'd rather be with Patricio, I'd hardly be here with you.' She slid both hands under her hair at the back, lifting it to allow the breeze to cool her nape. 'This is wonderful. There are so few days in England when an open-topped car is practical.'

'You own a car yourself?' Marcos asked.

'A very temperamental one,' she acknowledged laughingly. 'On cold mornings it's touch and go whether I finish up going to work on the bus!'

'You have no friends with more reliable vehicles to call upon for a lift?'

'None who live close enough.' Which was true enough, she defended. The one time she had rung Scott, he had made the point that by the time he had detoured to pick her up they would both be late for work.

Scott. Guilt assailed her once more, her only comfort in the thought that he deserved better than anything she could have given him to start with. She had to straighten things out with him the moment she got back.

Right now, going home was the last thing she wanted to think about. She stole a glance at the man at her side, devouring the hard-edged profile. Open at the throat, the scarlet shirt suited his dark looks. In another life he would have made a wonderful pirate, she thought dreamily. She could imagine him strutting the poop deck—wherever that was—brandishing a cutlass.

'What do you find so amusing?' he asked, and she realised she was smiling.

'I'm just happy,' she declared, throwing caution to the winds. 'Who wouldn't be on a day like this, riding in a car like this?'

'With a man no other can equal,' he appended straight-faced.

'That too, of course,' she agreed, and drew a laugh.

'You learn fast, *chica*.'

'I have the best of teachers,' she rejoined. 'And the very finest curriculum!'

They were coming up to the bend which preceded the village turn-off. Marcos drew in to the side of the road and killed the engine, pulling her to him to kiss her with an ardour that elicited instant and like response.

'Damn gearsticks!' she exclaimed breathlessly when he finally let her go. 'They really get in the way!'

'The next time I'll make certain to drive an automatic shift,' said Marcos amusedly. 'Never have I known a woman quite like you!'

'Of course you haven't,' she responded in mock indignation. 'I'm as unique in my way as you are in yours.'

He smiled, brushing the wind-tumbled hair back from her face. 'You find me so very different from your own countrymen?'

'As chalk is from cheese,' she confirmed, willing herself to stay on top of the emotions his very touch aroused in her.

'You've never truly loved a man?'

The question sent a quiver right through her. Her voice when she answered seemed to be coming from outside herself. 'I once believed I did.'

'What happened to make you realise it wasn't so?'

'I just realised, that's all.'

'And the man?'

Nicole crossed her fingers mentally, wishing she'd kept her mouth shut in the first place. 'He soon found someone else.'

'So, no hearts were broken.'

'No.' She forced a lighter note. 'How about you?'

He gave a smiling shrug. 'My heart remains whole too.'

And perhaps always would, Nicole thought as he turned away to start the engine again. If he married Elena it would probably be because she fulfilled his requirements; love didn't necessarily enter into it.

Awkward though it was going to be to face Patricio when they got back, Nicole deemed any further protest a waste of breath when it became obvious that they were indeed heading for the city. It was, she decided, up to Marcos to sort things out with his brother. In the meantime she was happy to just go along.

Filling a shallow basin between two forested mountain ranges, Caracas was a city of broad avenues and tree-lined plazas, its modern apartment and office blocks almost wholly obliterating the old Spanish and French architecture. The traffic was horrendous. Nicole was bound to acknowledge a certain relief at not having to tackle it on her own.

Marcos insisted that they do as she had planned and make her call on the agency, which turned out to be situated in a pedestrianised plaza. Nicole would have hesitated to leave the Ferarri unattended on a city-centre side street, but he showed no concern. If it was stolen it would either be recovered or replaced, she supposed.

He accompanied her into the agency, taking a seat at the rear to study a couple of brochures while she introduced herself to the counter staff. Her main contact here was a Mariá Merida, who turned out to be a good twenty years older than her voice had suggested, but whose delight on realising who Nicole was was instant.

'Never did I think to meet with you at any time!' she exclaimed. 'You are here on vacation yourself?'

It would have been simpler to say yes and leave it at that, but Nicole gave way to a sudden impulse. 'I'm here for the Peraza wedding,' she said. 'You might have heard the name.'

Mariá's eyes had opened wider. 'Of course. Everyone knows the name of Peraza! The wedding is much spoken of. You are a relative of the bride?'

This time it was definitely simpler to just say yes.

'And your companion?' she asked, with a conjectural glance in Marcos's direction. 'He is one of the family?'

'The elder son.' Faced with the obvious speculation, Nicole wished she'd kept her mouth shut. She was relieved when the outer doors opened to admit a small influx of people to join those already being attended to by other staff. 'Anyway, it looks like you're going to be busy, so I'll get out of your way. Lovely to have met you, Mariá.'

'And I you,' the other echoed, looking disappointed. 'Perhaps you will pay another, longer visit?'

'If I can,' Nicole promised, doubting if she would have the opportunity.

A client closed in as she turned away, commanding attention with what sounded like a complaint. Already on his feet, Marcos returned the brochures to the stand and went to open the door for her.

'It would hardly seem worth the trouble of coming at all for such a short conversation,' he remarked.

'There really didn't seem all that much to say when it came down to it,' Nicole admitted. 'I'm sorry for dragging you along.'

'I'm not in the habit of being *dragged* anywhere!' he remonstrated with mock severity.

'Especially by a woman,' she returned, tongue in cheek. 'I must remember to choose my words more carefully.'

'It may save misunderstanding,' he agreed. 'Are you hungry now?'

Not for food, she thought, vibrantly responsive to every lithe movement as he strode at her side. She wondered what his reaction would be if she told him what was uppermost in her mind right now.

'Some,' she said, opting on the side of discretion. 'Can we make it back in time for lunch?'

His shrug was light. 'There is no rule that says we must all sit to table at the same moment, but we shall be lunching here in the city.'

Nicole had no argument with that. She had no argument with anything that meant spending time together.

They arrived back at the car to find it under the surveillance of a small gang of raggedly-clothed and none too clean urchins. They'd been keeping an eye on it to make sure no one caused any damage, they claimed. Marcos handed over what appeared to Nicole to be a sizeable sum of money, drawing smiles all round.

'Insurance,' he said in answer to Nicole's unspoken query as the group melted rapidly away. 'There are many such gangs who come down from the *ranchos*. Refuse to pay, and the vehicle registration number will be passed along for future attention of a much less caring nature.'

The *ranchos*, Nicole knew, were the sprawling slums of tin sheds and cardboard boxes that covered the lower slopes. Product of the uncontrolled surge of post-war immigration, she had read.

'It amounts to blackmail!' she stated as he put her into the car.

'It amounts to survival,' came the matter-of-fact reply. 'Would you prefer to eat national or international?'

Nicole took the hint. As an outsider, none of it was her concern. 'National, please,' she said on a subdued note.

The restaurant he chose was rather more down-market than she would have anticipated, though both food and wine proved excellent. Marcos drank very little, she noted. Recalling the effect it had had on her yesterday lunchtime, she tempered her own intake. There was no knowing what she might let out under the influence!

She found that forbearance of little help when he started showing an interest in her home life. If ever there was a time to come clean about Scott it was now, but she couldn't bear to see disgust dawn in the dark eyes.

It was going to be hard enough telling Scott it was all off when she did get home. He was naturally going to want to know what had made her change her mind— especially as she had given no prior indication that she might be having second thoughts. One thing she would be keeping to herself was this affair—if it could be called that—with Marcos. It had little bearing on the decision anyway.

'Nicole?' Marcos was studying her quizzically. 'Are you here with me, or somewhere else?'

She shook herself mentally, dredging up a smile. 'I was thinking how cold it's going to feel back home after this. You don't know how lucky you are to have year-round sunshine!'

'We do suffer cool and cloudy days—even wet days,' he said. 'Is the weather the only advantage my country has over your own?'

'I'm hardly going to be here long enough to make that kind of judgement,' she rejoined.

There was a momentary pause before he answered, neither tone nor expression giving much away. 'So extend your stay.'

CHAPTER SEVEN

HEART thudding suddenly and painfully against her rib-cage, Nicole gazed across the table, trying to penetrate the impenetrable. 'Are you serious?'

Dark brows lifted in faint mockery. 'Why should I not be serious?'

'I have a job to get back to,' she said after a moment.

'Of course.' There was nothing in his tone to suggest regret. 'I was forgetting. So we must take full advantage of what time we have left to us.'

'We don't seem to have wasted all that much up to now,' she observed wryly.

Marcos reached across the table and took her hand, raising it to his lips. 'We were driven by the same overpowering need. The need I feel stirring my loins even now.' Amusement lit his eyes as she attempted to pull away. 'You showed no such reticence last night.'

'That was…different.' Nicole could feel the heat rising under her skin. 'People are looking at us!'

'Of course.' He was gently caressing her palm with the ball of his thumb, increasing her pulse-rate by the second. 'We make an eye-catching pair!'

'Modesty doesn't figure largely in your make-up, does it?' It was weak, but the best she could come up with. 'Aren't you afraid of being recognised?'

The dark brows lifted again. 'Why should I fear recognition?'

'For what the gossips might make of all this.'

He gave a laugh. 'They would have little enough to talk about! However, the likelihood is remote.'

'Because the people who might recognise you are hardly likely to be found in this neighbourhood?'

Marcos released her hand, humour suddenly vanished. 'You believe I brought you here because I was reluctant to be seen with you?'

She held his gaze, an element of challenge in the tilt of her chin. 'I doubt if it's a regular haunt.'

'Regular, no. I'm rarely in the city at this hour.' He registered her change of expression with a sardonic smile. 'The food is good, the service efficient, the ambience pleasant. What more is needed?'

'Sorry.' Nicole felt thoroughly mortified. 'I thought—'

'You thought wrongly.'

She bit her lip as he put up a hand to summon the waiter, aware of having angered him. If she'd had the sense she was born with, she would have realised they were neither of them dressed for the classier establishments.

She waited until they were in the car before attempting to rebuild bridges.

'Are we going to fall out over a silly misunderstanding?' she asked on what she hoped was the right note.

'Fall out?' Marcos looked momentarily baffled.

'Quarrel, then.' She sought the word in Spanish. '*Reñir.*'

'Children quarrel,' he said. 'I forgive you.'

Nicole shot him a swift glance, seeing the twitch at the corners of his mouth. 'That's very generous of you.'

He inclined his head. 'I see no sense in allowing a misunderstanding to come between us either.'

Particularly if it meant forgoing any further intimacies, she reflected with a cynical edge. She wondered how he would react if she locked her door against him tonight.

It wasn't going to happen, of course. She lacked the strength of mind to say no to her own urges, much less his. The danger lay in her inability to stay emotionally detached. She was already in far too deep.

There was no sign of Patricio when they got back.

'He stormed off somewhere after I told him you'd gone with Marcos,' said Leonora when Nicole sought her out on the terrace. 'Not to be wondered at, really.'

Nicole looked at her suspiciously. 'What else did you tell him.'

'I didn't need to tell him. He's obviously only too well accustomed to having his brother steal a march on him. He took great heart from the way you more or less ignored Marcos the first evening. The poor boy didn't realise it was tactical.'

'You really do like stirring it, don't you?' Nicole said shortly. 'There were no tactics involved.'

Her stepmother gave a smiling shrug. 'Whatever you say, darling. Where did you get to anyway? We were expecting you back for lunch.'

'We had lunch in Caracas.'

'Worse and worse! That's where Patricio wanted to take you.' Leonora held up a hand in mock defence. 'All right! All right! I won't mention him again. You're going to have trouble enough pacifying Scott. He rang about half an hour ago. Lucky I was around to take the call. He seems to think there's something odd going on. Said you rang him in the middle of the night.'

'The middle of the night here, first thing in the morning there.' Nicole hesitated. 'You didn't—?'

'Give me credit for *some* diplomacy. I told him you were out and I'd pass on the message. He'll be waiting to hear from you.'

Nicole ran a distracted hand through her hair. I can't do it now. I need a shower.'

'It's already around eight-thirty over there,' Leonora warned. 'You have to talk to him some time, so why not get on with it? If you're planning on going back to him, you need to set his mind at rest. Tell him how much you love him and all that!'

Nicole turned away, unable to meet the blue eyes. 'There's plenty of time.'

Marcos had gone over to the stables. She hoped he would run into Patricio and get things sorted. She had more than enough on her plate already. Scott deserved to know the truth, but not over the phone. That was the coward's way out.

'Incidentally,' Leonora called after her, 'I forgot to tell you this morning, but we're invited to the Laniezes' tonight. It's informal, so that green thing will do—unless you'd like to take another look through my wardrobe.'

Halted in the *salón* doorway, Nicole said expressionlessly, 'Do I really need to go?'

'It would be considered very discourteous if you didn't.' Her stepmother's voice had sharpened. 'Why wouldn't you want to go?'

Nicole could have told her in a word: Elena.

'Just a bit tired,' she said. 'Don't worry. I'll ginger myself up.'

She continued on indoors, summoning a few light words for the young maidservant she passed in the hall. The bedroom was a haven, if only a temporary one. As Leonora had said, she had to make the call some time.

Scott was far from obtuse; he already sensed something wrong. Perhaps it would be better after all to let him know where he stood right away.

Easier was what she really meant, she thought ruefully.

It was still only half past five when she emerged from the shower. Half past nine in England, conscience reminded her. If she left it much longer, Scott might ring back himself—this time with Marcos in the vicinity.

There was no one about when she went downstairs. Regretting the lack of privacy, she put the call through on the hall extension. Scott sounded abrupt.

'About time too! I was beginning to wonder if you were going to bother at all.'

'Sorry,' she said. 'We were late getting back.'

'Oh, yes, you were out with this Marcos.' The pause was weighty. 'Just the two of you, was it?'

'Yes.' Nicole was hard put to it to keep an even tone. 'He ran me into the city to visit the agency.'

'And that took all day?'

'We had lunch out too.' She hesitated, still not certain of how best to handle things. 'Scott, we need to…talk.'

Silence greeted the announcement. When he finally spoke it was in a different tone. 'Talk about what, exactly?'

Nicole drew in a hard breath. 'Us.'

'Just *what* are you trying to tell me?' He sounded well and truly disturbed now.

'I think we made a mistake,' she got out.

'In what sense?'

He obviously wasn't going to make things easy for her, she reflected wryly. But then, why should he?

'Every sense,' she said. 'We just don't have enough in common. You don't want children, for one thing.'

'I thought you were in agreement with that?'

'No. Just reluctant to make an issue of it at the time.'

'Well, I suppose that's something we do need to discuss, then.' He paused, as if expecting something more from her, his tone altered again when he spoke. 'There's more to it than that, isn't there? Leonora's talked you into this! She never did like me!'

It was ironic, Nicole thought, that he should accuse her stepmother in the same words she had used against him. 'It has nothing to do with Leonora,' she said. 'I just realised I'd been living a lie this past few months. It isn't you, Scott, it's me. I'm not ready to…marry anyone.'

'Not unless they come with a fortune attached, you mean!' His voice rasped with acrimony. 'I should have known what you had in mind when you insisted on going out there. Like mother, like daughter!'

'She's my stepmother. There's no blood connection.' Nicole was doing her best to stay in control. 'I've about as much chance of following in her footsteps as I have of entering the Olympics, so you can forget that angle.'

'I don't believe you!'

'I can't help that.' Feeling absolutely wretched, she said, 'I know I should have waited to tell you face to face, but it would have meant putting on a pretence every time I spoke to you on the phone. I'm sorry, Scott. Really and truly sorry. I'll see you when I get back.'

Movement above initiated a hasty replacement of the receiver. Descending the stairs, Patricio eyed her accusingly.

'Why have you encouraged my advances when you have no interest of that nature in me?' he demanded.

'I haven't encouraged you,' Nicole denied. 'Not intentionally, at any rate. 'I like you, Patricio. Very much. But—'

'But it's my brother who attracts you.' It was a statement not a question, tone more philosophical than hurt.

Nicole hesitated. It was obvious that Marcos had said something to his brother, but doubtful, if she read him right, that he would have revealed just how close their association was.

'I hear we're to dine out tonight,' she said, deeming it best to treat the question as rhetorical. 'Just a casual affair, Leonora tells me.'

Descended now to her level, Patricio lifted his shoulders. 'There is casual and casual.'

'That's helpful,' Nicole remarked drily. 'I take it trousers and shirts will only be worn by the men, but what would be considered suitable in my case?'

He looked her over, the wicked glint back in his eyes. 'Less is more—isn't that what all the fashion people say?'

'It depends how much less. The last thing I want is to show you all up.'

'You could never do that. Dressed in rags, your beauty would still outshine all others!'

Nicole had to laugh. 'You're a born flatterer, but useless as an advisor! I'll use my own judgement.'

'The dress you wore the other evening will be very suitable,' he said, adopting a sober note. 'Green enhances your colouring—not quite as much as the silver, perhaps, but that would certainly be too much for this occasion.' He bent suddenly forward and kissed her swiftly on the lips, expression innocent. 'If I'm to treat you like a sister I'm allowed certain familiarities.'

'Who said—?' Nicole began, breaking off abruptly on sight of Marcos standing in the archway leading through to the *salón*. Judging from his expression, he found the byplay anything but amusing.

Patricio looked unconcerned. He'd probably known Marcos was there all the time, Nicole conjectured. His way of getting back at big brother.

'Leonora has a fresh pot of hot tea ready, if you feel in need,' Marcos advised.

'Lovely.' Nicole refused to let the fear that her voice might have carried through to the *salón* gain a hold. She hadn't been speaking loudly enough on the phone. 'Are you a tea-drinker too?'

'I leave that kind of self-sacrifice to my father.' He watched her approach, eyes following the slender curves of her figure in the simple cotton tunic. 'You know we have an engagement tonight?'

Which one? it was on the tip of her tongue to murmur in passing, but she controlled the urge. 'I know,' she confirmed. 'I was asking Patricio's advice on what to wear.'

'Which I was supplying in proper brotherly fashion,' declared the latter at her back. 'I might try some of Leonora's tea myself for once.'

'I'll leave you to it,' said Marcos drily.

Nicole kept a smile on her face as she moved on into the room. She'd had most of the day with him, she chided herself, and there was still the night to come. What more did she want?

She shied away from the all too obvious answer.

Costly though the green dress had been, it didn't begin to compare with those worn by the Laniez women—or Leonora either. Nicole refused to let it concern her. Those who could afford haute couture wore haute couture; those who couldn't didn't.

What did matter to her, despite her every effort not to let it, was the way in which Elena managed to monopolise Marcos from the moment they arrived. Not that he appeared in any way disinclined to be monopolised, she had to admit.

She wasn't the only one nursing a bad case of green eye. Isabella didn't even attempt to conceal it. Three women all yearning for the same man—with hers by far the least likely to bear fruit.

They ate at nine, afterwards retiring to a *salón* no less grand than the one at Las Veridas for coffee and liqueurs. Probably another couple of hours to go before any move was made towards leaving, Nicole judged with a surreptitious glance at her watch. She didn't think she could stand it till then.

Patricio was seated at her side, though with rather more space between them than he might have claimed before Marcos had said his piece.

'How come you don't fancy Isabella yourself?' she asked him lightly, for want of anything else to say.

He gave a shrug, eyes suddenly veiled. 'Isabella has many admirers, but she has eyes for no one but Marcos.'

'But she isn't going to get him, is she?' Nicole gave the knife a masochistic twist. 'Not while Elena's around.'

'If Marcos marries Elena, then Isabella will need to look elsewhere, yes,' he agreed.

'You think it likely, then?'

'Possible. The only one who knows for certain is Marcos himself. He doesn't take me into his confidence.' Patricio gave her a sideways look. 'It matters to you?'

Nicole tried a shrug herself. 'Why should it? I'll be gone in a few days.'

'It means nothing at all, then, this affair with my brother?'

For a frozen moment Nicole could find no answer. 'He told you?' she managed at length.

Patricio shook his head. 'You just confirmed the suspicion he aroused this afternoon when he told me I was to make no further approaches towards you.'

'He had no right to do that,' Nicole protested weakly.

'If it's true that you are lovers already, then he had every right.'

Green eyes searched dark ones, finding no visible censure. 'You must hold a very low opinion of me now.'

Patricio smiled briefly. 'Why should a woman not enjoy the same freedom to indulge her desires as a man?'

'Including your own women?'

'Some of them, perhaps.'

'But you'd prefer the one you married to be untouched, of course.'

'That would depend on my reasons for marrying. If it was for love, I could forget others that might have gone before me.'

'Supposing you never find that kind of love?'

Just for a moment there was bleakness in his eyes, though his tone remained easy. 'If I reach the age Marcos is without it happening, I shall marry the most suitable virgin I can find and raise fine sons instead.'

'How about daughters?'

'Not unless it proved inevitable. I hear there are ways of ensuring the sex of a child at conception.'

'I wouldn't place too much reliance on it. What's wrong with girls, anyway?'

'They become women.'

Nicole let the remark pass, already beginning to suspect the possible underlying cause. 'How do *you* really feel about the wedding, Patricio?' she asked, sidetracking for the moment.

'When I see Father looking the way he has since bringing Leonora home, I can only be happy for him,' he returned.

'So you find nothing wrong with the way they met?'

'If something is meant to be, it will happen. The fates decreed that your stepmother should step into the street at the exact time that my father was passing. A moment earlier or later and they would neither of them ever have known.'

'It's a good thing he was able to stop before actually hitting her. What was he driving?'

'The Lamborghini, I believe. He and Marcos share an enthusiasm for fast cars.

It was fortunate that the traffic was heavy enough to curtail his speed.'

Perhaps even to the point where Leonora would have had time to assess both car and driver before stepping out, Nicole cogitated for a brief moment, immediately dismissing the idea. She had to stop allowing Marcos's suspicions to rub off on her and start believing, like Patricio, that fate had ordained events. It didn't matter, anyway, providing no one finished up getting hurt.

The one most likely to do that was herself, she reflected. Her own fault; she should have stayed home where she belonged. She cast a glance across the room to where Marcos and Elena appeared to be deep in conversation. 'Possible', Patricio had said in reference to marriage between the two of them, yet surely no man would have the face to bring lover and future wife together in the same room?

Whether or not, it was time to get a grip on herself, she resolved heavily. The affair, such as it was, had to finish right here before she became any more deeply enmeshed.

Confirmation of her earlier suspicion came when she looked back at Patricio to find him watching Isabella with an expression her heightened sensibilities couldn't fail to recognise. He switched his gaze immediately, donning his customary insouciant manner.

'So tell me about your work,' he invited.

'If you feel that way about her, why don't you do something about it?' Nicole asked softly. She shook her head as he began an obvious denial. 'I saw you. Only for a second, but it was enough. Does she know?'

Patricio made a resigned gesture. 'You're the only one who knows. I hope it will remain that way.'

'I've no intention of telling anyone,' she assured him. 'How long have you loved her?'

'Since she was just a schoolgirl,' he admitted. 'For her there has never been anyone but Marcos.'

'But there are fourteen years between them.'

'Years matter little to the heart. She lives in hope that he'll pass Elena by and choose her instead. There's little chance of it, but while he remains unwed she will continue to wait.'

'You've never attempted to tell her how you feel?'

'It would be no use. She regards me in the same way she would regard a brother.'

'So give her reason to take another look.' Nicole was

warming to the cause—partly because it took her mind off the two across the way.

The smile was faint. 'I have tried. It makes no impact on her when I pay attention to others.'

Green eyes took on sudden enlightenment. 'Including me, I take it?'

'Including you,' he agreed, looking just a little sheepish. 'Not that I had much success in claiming *your* attention in competition with my brother either.'

There was nothing Nicole could say to that. It was only too true. 'All the same, I wouldn't give up all hope,' she encouraged. 'The way Isabella keeps looking over here, she's none too keen on you being with me right now.'

'You think so?' He sounded a fraction more upbeat.

'I'd say definitely.' Nicole was more inclined to put the hostility down to general rancour towards herself than jealousy, but he needed all the encouragement he could get if he was to stand any chance of ousting his brother where Isabella was concerned.

On impulse, she took hold of his hand, turning it over to view his palm. 'Let me read your lines and tell you what the future holds for you.'

'You study palmistry?' he asked, intrigued.

'I've done a little.' A very little, would have been closer the truth, her sole attempt having been under the influence of a drink or two too many at some party. 'You've a strong heartline,' she continued. 'And a very long lifeline. I see four, no *five* children—perhaps even six! Looks like you're going to be pretty busy, anyway.'

'You,' he said laughingly, 'are a fraud! I don't believe a word of it!'

She wrinkled her nose at him. 'Oh, ye of little faith!

They had become the focus of attention from several people in the vicinity, she realised suddenly—Marcos no exception. Her first inclination was to drop Patricio's hand like a hot potato, but she resisted it, folding his fingers over his palm without haste. 'If Isabella is worth having, she's worth fighting for,' she declared in low tones. 'It's up to you.'

It was gone one when they finally left. Driving the same silver limousine in which he had picked her up from the airport, Marcos had them back at Las Veridas within twenty minutes. Nicole proved the only dissenter when Leonora proposed a nightcap before retiring.

'I'll go straight up, if no one minds,' she said, smothering a fake yawn. 'I can hardly keep my eyes open as it is.'

She made her escape before anyone could comment, carefully avoiding so much as a glance in Marcos's direction. There was a lock on her bedroom door. Turning the key was an emotional if not a physical effort—the urge to turn it back again almost too much for her. The only thing stopping her was the knowledge that she was heading for a dead end where Marcos was concerned. Come the end of the week, she would be the only loser.

As it turned out, she needn't have bothered because he didn't come near. Either he'd decided to play fair by Elena or he'd simply lost interest in pursuing the affair any further, Nicole surmised. Either way, the situation was resolved.

Morning found her in a frame of mind to head for home, but it was impossible to come up with any plausible reason for leaving before the wedding. The only face-saving alternative, she decided, was to act as if

nothing had ever happened between her and Marcos—
to treat him, in effect, with the indifference she had
first intended. No easy task considering what *had* happened between them.

The reality proved even harder than anticipated, the
smile and easy *'Buenas días'* with which he greeted
her at breakfast like rubbing salt into a raw wound.
Whatever he was feeling, regret certainly didn't figure
very largely.

'I trust you are rested?' queried Eduardo solicitously
as she helped herself to coffee. 'Tonight we shall stay
home and enable you to retire at an earlier hour. It
takes time to adjust to new ways.'

'If you'd taken a siesta yesterday afternoon, instead
of gallivanting all over Caracas, you might have managed to last out the evening better,' said Leonora. 'You
should have had more thought, Marcos.'

The dark head inclined with a hint of mockery. 'I
should indeed.'

'I'm fine,' Nicole assured Eduardo. 'I slept like a
top.'

Which was no lie, she reflected cynically; she'd
spent half the night tossing and turning. She took a
seat, aware of Marcos's eyes on her. If he expected her
to be aggrieved over last night's seeming neglect, he
could think again. She had herself well in hand.

'How about going for a ride this morning?' she
asked Patricio with deliberation, ignoring the twinge in
her nether regions. 'There's a whole lot of countryside
I've still to see.'

The latter darted a glance at his brother, who returned it expressionlessly. 'It would be my pleasure,'
he agreed after a moment.

'Always providing I can borrow your things again, of course?' Nicole added to Leonora.

'You've still got them from the last time,' her step-mother pointed out. 'Lucky I'm not reliant on the one outfit.'

Looking from one to the other of his sons, Eduardo seemed on the verge of making some observation, then apparently changed his mind and asked Leonora if she would like to drive into Caracas for luncheon instead.

Nicole concentrated her attention on the cup in her hand. With the two of them out of the way, it was going to be difficult to avoid being alone with Marcos at some point, but so what? A woman of the world, he had called her; that was the role she intended playing.

Having arranged to meet Patricio at the stables, she was in the bedroom changing into riding gear when Leonora came in without bothering to knock.

'What went wrong?' she asked bluntly.

Nicole kept her expression carefully neutral. 'What are you talking about?'

'You know very well what I'm talking about!' her stepmother snorted. 'Yesterday the two of you were all over one another; this morning you give him the cold shoulder and Patricio the come-on. If you're thinking of playing one off against the other, I wouldn't.'

'I'm not,' Nicole denied. 'I asked Pat to go for a ride, that's all.'

'Leaving Marcos sitting there with egg on his face.'

Nicole finished pulling on the boots, head bent. 'Why the sudden concern for *his* feelings? I didn't think you liked him all that much.'

'Considering that we're going to be sharing a home for the foreseeable future, I'm prepared to make an effort.' There was a pause as she waited for some response, a sudden change of tone. 'You've fallen for him, haven't you? I mean well and truly!'

Nicole came abruptly upright, colour staining her cheeks. 'Don't be ridiculous!'

'I should have known you were talking through your hat with all that stuff about having a fling!' Leonora continued as if she hadn't spoken. 'You've never been the type. I take it he's not thinking long-term himself?'

'He's not thinking anything,' Nicole said flatly. 'He's going to marry Elena.'

'He's told you that?'

'He doesn't need to. You saw the two of them together last night.'

'I saw her hanging onto him like grim death, if that's what you mean.'

Nicole gave a faint smile. 'He seemed happy enough to be hung onto.'

'He couldn't do much about it without being discourteous. In any case, there's no official betrothal, so the field's still wide open.'

'It can stay that way for me,' Nicole declared. 'I should have had more sense in the first place.'

'Except that sense takes a back seat when the sap starts rising,' observed her stepmother. 'I'd be willing to lay a bet Scott never turned you on the same way!'

'Leave Scott out of it.' Nicole had had enough. 'In fact, leave it altogether, will you?'

'Fine.' Leonora lifted her shoulders resignedly. 'As I've said before, some people you just can't help. Enjoy your ride.'

Nicole stifled the impulse to apologise for her acerbity. Leonora would only take it as a sign of weakened resolve. Alone again, she finished getting ready. If she owed anyone an apology, it was Patricio, for putting him in an awkward situation the way she had just to save her precious pride. It was time she faced up to her mistakes like an adult.

CHAPTER EIGHT

SHE FOUND Rojo already tacked up and waiting. The groom holding him said the master would be with her in a moment. Only when the grey stallion clattered into view did she realise *which* master.

'Patricio had other matters to attend to,' said Marcos without particular inflection. 'He sends his apologies.'

Nicole steeled herself to look him in the eye. 'Too bad.'

She turned the gelding without further ado and headed for the archway leading out from the spacious yard, keeping a tight rein on both mount and emotions. If Marcos thought he could play fast and loose with her as the fancy took him, he'd made a big mistake.

He caught up with her on the rough track, drawing alongside.

'Could it be that my forbearance last night was misplaced?' he asked levelly. 'Or do you have other reasons for treating me with disdain this morning?'

Nicole jerked her head round to look at him in sudden disorientation. 'Forbearance?'

'You gave the impression of being too tired to welcome my attentions.'

'Oh?' It was all she could think of to say at that moment, her mind in overdrive. No deliberate rejection but a thoughtful gesture; that was what he was implying. The kind of gesture she would never have expected from him.

126

'Oh?' Marcos lifted a quizzical eyebrow. 'Is that your only comment?'

She made an effort to bring her thoughts to order. Thoughtful gesture, maybe, but it didn't really change anything. She was still his bit on the side—the all too easy English conquest who would soon be gone from his life. Her decision to turn him away last night had been the right one; she couldn't afford to go back on it now.

'I appreciate the sentiment,' she got out, 'but it wasn't tiredness I was feeling last night. I'd already decided to call it a day.' She winced inwardly at the unintentional pun. 'Best all round.'

'*I* will decide what is best for *me*,' he returned with force. 'When exactly was this decision of yours made?'

Her shrug was meant to convey cool detachment. 'Does it matter?'

'If the time I spent with Elena last evening was the crux, then, yes.'

Nicole gave a short laugh. 'You're entitled to spend your time any way you see fit. So, for that matter, am I. This morning I fancied your brother's company.'

'This morning you put him in a very difficult position,' came the terse reply.

'Why? Because you'd told him I was *your* property?'

They had come to the point where the track split, one branch heading back towards the *casa*, the other into the encroaching woodland. Marcos leaned over and grasped Rojo's rein close up by the bit, bringing both horses to a stop. His face was set, his eyes glittering with barely held in anger.

'As the one you chose to bestow your favours on, I was entitled to claim dominion!'

Face flaming, Nicole took refuge in an anger of her own. 'Not where I come from!'

'But you are not where you come from,' he said, his accent suddenly more pronounced. 'You are here in my country, where the codes of conduct are very different. If you wished our relationship to go no further, you had only to tell me.'

'I just did!' she retorted.

'Not in any honourable manner.'

'You're a fine one to talk!' Nicole was past keeping the act going, her knuckles white where they clutched the rein, her pulses hammering. 'An honourable man would have married Elena by now, or made it clear that he had no intention. Instead you allow her to go on waiting and hoping. What is it—a sop to your vanity to have her fawning around you? And not just Elena either. You've got Isabella on the same string.'

Marcos gazed at her in silence for several taut seconds, his expression indecipherable. When he finally spoke it was with control. 'I've given neither Elena nor Isabella reason to look to me for marriage.'

'Not in so many words, perhaps, but from what I've seen you don't put much effort into discouraging the pair of them.'

'You've met Isabella on three occasions in my company, Elena on just the two,' he said. 'You consider that enough to prove me a philanderer?'

'Taking last night's performance into account, it's more than enough.' Nicole could have bitten off her tongue the moment the over-hasty words left her lips, seeing the angry glitter give way to sudden comprehension. 'Among other things,' she tagged on lamely.

'So I was right,' he said on an altogether softer note.

'It aroused you to jealousy to see me paying attention to another woman.'

'It made me realise what kind of man you really are,' she retorted, grasping at straws. 'I must have been mad letting you near me in the first place! I didn't like you when we met, and I like you even less now!'

'An insipid term at the best of times.' Marcos was smiling, eyes gently mocking. 'What we share, you and I, is passion, *querida*—among other things. Last evening, when you were speaking so intimately with my brother, I felt the pangs of jealousy myself.'

Sinking fast, Nicole made a last-ditch attempt to bail out. 'Not enough to stir you into leaving Elena.'

'Courtesy alone deprived me of the ability to do that. There is no arrangement between us, and never will be, as well she knows.'

Green eyes registered uncertainty. 'If she knows, why does she still hang on?'

'Perhaps because she believes perseverance may eventually wear down my resistance. I'm far from being her only hope of making a good marriage—although if she wastes much more time she may find herself with a very limited choice.'

'Love being the last consideration, of course.'

Broad shoulders lifted. 'It should by no means be the only consideration if a marriage is to last.

Quiet up until now, the stallion made a sudden sideways movement, sparking off a nervous skitter on Rojo's part. Marcos was forced to release his grasp on the gelding's rein in order to bring his own mount back under control, leaving Nicole to grapple with an animal who appeared to have decided that a return to base might be a good idea.

He didn't get very far. Marcos simply turned the grey across to block him.

'The fault was mine for allowing my attention to be distracted,' he said. 'Plata takes advantage of any lapse.' He paused, eyes penetrating her defences. 'You wish to continue?'

He could mean the ride alone, but Nicole doubted it. If she said yes, she would be agreeing to the whole caboodle. Even if she accepted his word over Elena, it left her in no better position than she had been before.

Yet what more could she expect? He was hardly likely to emulate his father and offer her his undying love. The choice was a straight one: a few more days—and nights—of physical if not emotional closeness, or nothing.

Put that way…

'Why not?' she said, and found a smile to go with it, albeit a spurious one. 'It's what we started out to do.'

'We started out on the wrong leg, as you would say,' Marcos returned.

'Foot,' she corrected, the smile genuine this time. 'As you well know!'

He laughed. 'A slip of the tongue. Where would you like to go?'

'Anywhere you want to take me,' she said, abandoning caution. 'I'm entirely in your hands.'

So much for indifference, she reflected wryly, seeing the gleam spring into the dark eyes. They were back on track in every sense.

With so much woodland around, privacy was easily come by. Nicole slid down from the saddle into the waiting arms without hesitation, lifting a ready mouth to his.

Shaded from the sun, she felt the air cool on her skin, but not for long. He took her with an urgency that stirred like response, their mingled cries at the peak sending a whole flock of birds screeching into the air.

She knew now why it was called the small death, thought Nicole, regaining her senses. She felt born again, rejuvenated! She pressed loving lips to the dark head resting at her breast, feeling him stir.

'An hour ago, I was beginning to wonder if I might be mistaken after all,' he said softly, without lifting his head.

'About what?' she asked.

'Your feelings for me.'

'What kind of feelings are you talking about?' she managed after a lengthy moment.

Marcos gave a low laugh. 'The kind *I* believed myself immune from. When I came to meet you at the airport it was with the intention of putting you on the next flight back to England, but once having seen you I found it impossible.'

'Because you wanted me?' Her voice sounded thick.

'That, yes, but also because I had to discover the truth about you.'

Nicole swallowed on the dryness in her throat. 'And you think you have?'

He hoisted himself on an elbow, looking down at her with an expression she had never hoped to see in his eyes. 'I believe so. If you'd been of the same mind as your stepmother, you would have made every effort to engage my good opinion from the start rather than contend with me. True, there were moments when I suspected that you might have selected Patricio as the easier prey, but you proved my fears groundless in giving yourself to me instead of him.'

He waited, a faint line drawn between his brows when she failed to make any immediate reply. 'Am I so wrong in my assumptions?'

'I'm still not sure exactly what assumptions you're making,' Nicole forced out.

His mouth curved again. 'That we share the same desires, the same needs, the same temperament. We belong together, *querida*. Not just for the night or the day, but for life.'

He wasn't serious, Nicole thought dazedly, searching the vitally handsome face. He couldn't possibly be serious!

'It's been less than four days since we met,' she said. 'How can—?'

'Time has no bearing on affairs of the heart,' he declared. 'Mine has never been engaged before this.'

'Mine neither,' she whispered after a long moment of wrestling with her conscience. 'But…'

'But?' he prompted as she sought the words to tell him what she must tell him. 'Are you not prepared to follow your heart?'

If it weren't for what she knew there would be no hesitation, she thought painfully. To have Marcos feel the same way for her that she felt for him was beyond all expectation, but would those feelings survive the realisation that she'd concealed a fiancé from him?

It was doubtful, to say the least. The way he would probably see it was that his initial assessment had been right after all. So why take the risk? she asked herself. The only one here who knew about Scott was Leonora, and she was hardly likely to give her away. In any case, she'd already broken the engagement off, so what was the point in saying anything at all?

'Why do you hesitate?' Marcos asked, the frown returning as he watched the play of expression across her face. 'Do I not make my intentions towards you clear enough?'

'Not totally,' she said, taking the plunge. 'Are you suggesting I become your mistress?'

It was a moment before he answered, eyes impenetrable. 'You would accept that role?'

Hoping she hadn't misread the situation, Nicole shook her head. 'No way!'

'So it's marriage or nothing, you're saying?'

She took heart from the smile that accompanied the question, bringing up a hand to gently trace the firm lines of his mouth. 'Is it too much to ask for?'

'It's the only arrangement I have in mind,' he confirmed. 'I was lost from the moment I first laid eyes on you—although I did my best to conceal it, even from myself. Even if you'd proved to be less than the person you are, I would have found it difficult to turn away from you. I've waited all my adult life for a woman who could make me feel the way you make me feel.'

He ran a possessive gaze down the slender length of her body, following it with a lingering fingertip. Nicole felt her breath shorten again as he circled her breast, her thighs clenching in anticipation as the same tender touch drifted downwards. Time had no bearing on affairs of the heart, he had said, and hers was quite definitely engaged—along with every other part of her.

It was gone midday when they returned to the *casa*. With Eduardo and Leonora gone to Caracas, as planned, and Patricio having left no word as to his whereabouts, it was just the two of them at lunch. Afterwards, Marcos insisted that Nicole spend at least an hour or so resting in order to be fresh for the evening.

'Tonight I make no concessions,' he said.

'I wouldn't want you to,' Nicole assured him, still way up in the clouds. She gave a laugh. 'It's going to be a real shock for everyone. I'm not sure I even believe it myself yet. Why me?'

Looking at her as she stood there in the sunlight, her hair a flaming glory about her lovely face, Marcos shook his head in mock bafflement. 'I can think of no good reason.'

Taking in the superb physique and wonderfully modelled, masculine features, Nicole had no such problem. He put all other men in the shade.

It was only when she was alone in her dimmed bedroom that the problems began filtering in. There were so many things that would have to be sorted out. Unlike Leonora, she couldn't simply abandon everything back home. Her job, the flat—they all had to be dealt with. She hadn't even finished sorting out Leonora's own affairs.

There was Scott too, of course. She might have made a mistake in agreeing to marry him in the first place, but she owed him better than that hasty phone call. She had to face him, to try and make him understand the difference between what she felt for him and what she felt for Marcos.

He wouldn't, of course. He'd simply take it that she'd found a better prospect. All the same, it had to be gone through.

Hardly expecting to sleep with so much going on in her mind, she was surprised to open her eyes and find more than two hours had passed since she had come upstairs. Memory brought a smile to her lips—along with a determination not to let anything impinge on that happiness. Some time in the not too distant future she was going to be Marcos's wife. It was all she cared about right now.

She took a shower before dressing in one of the simple, though not so inexpensive cotton shifts she had deemed practical for the climate, this time in the palest turquoise patterned with a deeper-toned flower. Both eyes and hair seemed to have acquired an extra sheen, she thought, brushing the latter before the mirror. She looked—and felt—like someone with a lamp lit inside.

Marcos had said nothing about when and where the news was going to be broken to the others. Expecting to at least be there, Nicole was somewhat nonplussed by her stepmother's greeting when she joined the family gathering on the terrace.

'You certainly had me fooled, darling!' Leonora exclaimed. 'It was only this morning you were telling me there was no chance of you and Marcos making it this far. I never had you down for the impulsive kind either,' she added to her future stepson. 'It just goes to show that blood will out in the end!'

Eduardo came to take Nicole by the shoulders and kiss her on both cheeks, his pleasure obviously genuine, though tinged by a certain bemusement. 'I believed it was Patricio you favoured,' he said, 'but I'm delighted that one of my sons has managed to persuade you to stay with us. It may even be possible for the two of you to share our wedding day.'

Catching a glimpse of her stepmother's face over his shoulder, Nicole had to fight to keep her expression reasonably sober. 'A nice idea, but hardly practical,' she said, wondering what Marcos thought of it. 'I'm expected back at my job next week, for one thing.'

'And you have your flat, etcetera, to get rid of, of course,' Leonora agreed readily. 'Not that it should take long to organise. You could probably be back here soon after we return from honeymoon.'

'Matters will be taken care of,' said Marcos drily. He donned a smile as he met Nicole's eyes, indicating the tray residing on one of the low tables. 'The tea is freshly made. For the third time, I might add. I was about to come and find you.'

Patricio got to his feet as she moved forward, stepping up to emulate his father's greeting. 'Welcome to the family,' he said on a formal note, breaking into a grin as he surveyed her. 'You had me fooled too. Both of you!' he added, with a glance at his brother. 'Like Leonora, I'd never have believed you capable of impetuosity.'

'I surprise myself at times,' Marcos returned with a certain irony. He smiled at Nicole as she slid into a seat close by. 'But not this time. I'll come to England with you and help make the necessary arrangements. The apartment is your own property?'

She shook her head, too perturbed to think straight. 'It's on lease.'

'That simplifies matters. It should take no more than a week to finalise everything.'

'I have to give at least a month's notice at work,' she protested. 'I'm under contract.'

'That can be taken care of too.'

'So you may even be back before our return,' said Eduardo, obviously taking it for granted that the deed was as good as done. 'All that is needed now is for you to find a suitable match,' he added to his younger son.

Patricio gave a light shrug. 'Some day, perhaps.'

He was thinking that with Marcos no longer available he might at last stand a chance with Isabella, Nicole surmised, seeing the faint smile flicker across his lips. Except that there was every chance Marcos would be back on the market again when he found out about Scott. Which he would, of course, if he did as he had said and accompanied her back home.

Short of persuading him to let her go alone, which would call for reasons she couldn't even begin to come up with, her only option was to tell him the truth first. Yet, if she did, the chances of his turning against her were just as great.

Whichever way she handled it, he was unlikely to believe she'd been having doubts about marrying Scott before she'd even got here, she concluded cheerlessly. Faced with the same situation, she doubted if she'd believe it herself. All the same, she had to try. Only not right away. She had to choose the right moment— if there could ever be a right moment for something of this nature. Perhaps in a day or two, when she'd had chance to show him just how much he meant to her.

Catching her stepmother's eye, she gave a small, wry shrug. Leonora was the only one with any idea of what was going through her mind right now, though there was little help to be gained from that quarter. She couldn't lay the blame for it all entirely at her door either.

'You're looking very pensive,' Marcos observed. He regarded her with quizzically lifted brows. 'Am I allowed to know your thoughts?'

Nicole summoned a smile. 'I'm still finding it hard to take in. Four days ago at this time I was only just stepping off the plane.'

'It's a great deal longer than Eduardo and I took to

make up our minds,' Leonora put in. 'Why not follow my example and just leave everything, darling? There can't be much that's going to be of use out here anyway. All you need do is write and tell everyone you're not coming back. Marcos can take care of all the official stuff at this end, the way Eduardo did for me.'

For a moment, Nicole saw light at the end of the tunnel, but it soon faded. 'I didn't even get your flat emptied yet, much less mine,' she said hollowly.

'One of those house clearance firms would take care of all that. What they didn't want could go to charity.'

'It must all be done in a right and proper manner,' declared Marcos. 'I'll book a flight.'

This time it was Leonora who gave the wry little shrug, as if to say, Well, I tried! Nicole kept the smile going somehow. There was no way out of this but the truth. Eventually.

As promised, Marcos made no concessions to possible tiredness that night. He made no attempt to conceal the fact that they were spending the night together from the others either. So far as he was concerned, the wedding was just a formality, Nicole gathered; they had already plighted their troth.

She put heart and soul into her responses, letting go of all inhibition to match his every move. It was heaven to drift off to sleep exhausted in his arms, bliss to waken with renewed vigour to enjoy yet another sensual feast.

There was no room for forward thinking. No room for anything but pure sensation. She loved his strength, his purpose, the hard muscularity of his thighs trapped between her twined legs, the feel of him deep inside her. His hands were instruments of exquisite pleasure, seeking out erotic zones she hadn't even known existed until now, driving her wild in their mastery; his mouth was the same, leaving no part of her unexplored.

This time he stayed the whole night, waking at seven, when she could no longer resist the urge to touch him, to make love to her once more.

'Insatiable,' he said softly, when the frenzy had passed.

'Indefatigable,' Nicole responded, eyes closed in utter beatitude. 'You're a man and a half, Señor Peraza!'

'I'm going to need the strength of two men to keep my wife satisfied,' he laughed. 'Not that I would have her any other way, you understand.'

Green eyes came open again as memory encroached, but the euphoria refused to diminish. It would be all right. It had to be all right! Hadn't he said only yesterday that even if she'd proved to be less than the person he'd taken her to be, he would have found it difficult to turn away from her. Later today—or perhaps tomorrow—she would tell him about Scott.

The wedding service wasn't until two, but preparations were well under way by seven. Beautifully draped tables were laid around the courtyard, with the fountain as a centrepiece, and a shallow platform built to hold the musicians who would play both during and after the feast. Flowers festooned every niche, every corner, hanging in baskets, spilling from stone pots and urns, creating a riot of colour and a myriad of scents.

Time was fast running out, Nicole acknowledged ruefully at breakfast, watching the happily chattering staff at their tasks. With their flight now booked for the day after tomorrow, she had little more than forty-eight hours in which to find that elusive right moment to come clean about Scott. Even less than that, in reality, because she couldn't bring herself to do it today.

She stole a glance at Marcos, who was talking with Patricio. Much as she tried to convince herself that it would be all right in the end, the doubt was still there. Their relationship was based on very little more than physical attraction at present, when it came right down to it. It wouldn't take much to undermine such a foundation.

'All of this is soon to be repeated,' declared Eduardo expansively. 'And to think that a bare month ago we none of us had even the faintest notion of what was to happen.

'Fate moves in strange ways,' agreed Leonora, with no hint of satire in her voice for once.

'I take it you didn't get round to telling Marcos about Scott yet?' she said later, when she and Nicole were alone.

Nicole shook her head unhappily. 'I just never seem to find the right time.'

'You could try phoning Scott and putting him in the picture,' her stepmother suggested. 'If he's half the man you always say he is, he'll not try to spoil things for you.'

Unlikely, even if she hadn't already put him in the picture, Nicole reflected. Although he'd made no further attempt to contact her since she'd told him it was all off, he'd be round like a shot the moment he knew she was back, if not in the hope of changing her mind, at the very least to give her a piece of his. No more than she deserved either. She should never have agreed to marry him in the first place without being a hundred per cent sure it was what she really wanted.

There were no lingering doubts in her mind where

Marcos was concerned for certain. The very thought of being parted from him was anguish. Somehow she had to find a way of convincing him that she hadn't simply seen him as the better catch.

'I can see you think it as improbable as I do myself,' Leonora commented drily. 'In which case, you'll just have to rely on Marcos having enough feeling for you to forgive you.'

You're as much to blame as I am, Nicole wanted to say, but she knew it wasn't really true. It had been up to her to put the record straight. Marcos would certainly see it that way.

She put the whole matter firmly aside for the present. Another day would make no difference. For now, the wedding was the important thing.

Packed to the doors and beyond, the lovely old church was a perfect setting, the sun slanting through stained-glass windows onto wall paintings fit for a cathedral. Leonora had no attendants. The limelight, she had stated, belonged wholly to the bride. Her dress was a deep rich cream, embroidered all over with seed pearls, the neckline cut to sit proud on her fine shoulders, the skirt fitted to her slender waist and falling sheer to the tops of her cream brocade shoes.

Resplendent at her side in a tuxedo of deep garnet-red, Eduardo looked the proudest man on earth. They made a superbly handsome couple, thought Nicole, blinking back a tear or two at the memory of a previous wedding. Her father had been handsome too, and equally in love with his beautiful bride.

'Take this,' said Marcos softly, handing her a pristine white handkerchief as they came out from the church in the wake of the newly-weds. 'Shall you weep at our wedding too?'

She returned his smile with an effort, wondering if that day would really come. 'A feminine weakness,' she said, 'but I'll do my best to curtail it.'

'You are far from weak,' he responded. 'And no amount of weeping could dim your beauty.' He slanted a gaze over her long, body-skimming dress of amber wild silk, returning to devour every feature of her face beneath the wide brim of her pale apricot hat. 'My world will be complete on the day you become my wife, *querida*!'

'Mine too,' she said huskily, hoping against hope.

Eyes kindling, he took her hand, raising it to his lips. 'This evening, I shall make the formal announcement.'

'This is Leonora's and your father's day,' Nicole demurred in sudden panic. 'Perhaps we should wait for a better time.'

'It's my father's request,' he said. 'And what better time can there be than when everyone is gathered together?'

Nicole looked to where her stepmother and new husband were getting into the horse-drawn carriage that would transport them back to the *casa*. 'The Perazas certainly don't believe in hanging about,' was all she could find to say.

'We see no point in wasting time once a decision is made,' Marcos agreed.

He slid a hand about her waist to steer her through the throng to the waiting cars, returning greetings from all sides as they went. Nicole sensed the speculation aroused by their obvious togetherness, caught the occasional whispered comment. She was thankful to sink into the cushioned luxury of the limousine and be borne away from it all for a few minutes.

As always, Marcos was doing the driving. She

watched his hands on the wheel, the long, flexible fingers that could provide so much pleasure, the tendons lying just beneath the golden skin. The beautifully cut tuxedo outlined the powerful breadth of his shoulders, the deep blue colour wonderful against the coal-black of his hair.

One more night, she thought hungrily. One more night before she made the confession that might rob her of everything.

Using every available means of transport, the villagers followed the wedding party to the *casa*, spilling over the landscaped gardens in exuberant enjoyment of the food and drink provided. Guitars and violins were produced, filling the air with music to set the feet tapping.

Seated at table along with the other main guests, as the afternoon turned into evening, Nicole longed to be out there with the peasantry, mindful of nothing but having a good time. When Marcos finally rose to make the announcement she had to force herself to sit still, to smile at the astounded faces turned her way and accept the words of goodwill—spurious though some of them obviously were—with grace.

She felt even worse when Marcos produced a magnificent diamond and emerald ring and slid it onto her finger. It had been his mother's, he said softly. Left to him for this very purpose. It was a little loose, but it could be altered. In the meantime, he wished her to wear it.

Catching a glimpse of Elena's taut face alongside her sister's dispirited one, Nicole felt an empathic pang. It was still possible that she would prove a loser too.

Space was cleared for dancing. Urged by all, the bridal couple were the first to take to the floor. She hadn't seen Leonora looking as happy as this in a long time, thought Nicole, watching the pair of them slowly gyrate. Money might have some bearing on that happiness, but it was far from being the sole attraction.

'Shall we?' asked Marcos.

He took her agreement for granted, swinging her into his arms. Nicole laid her cheek against the broad chest, feeling the steady throb of his heart. Just this one night…

There was a commotion over by the doors leading through to the *salón*, the sound of voices raised in altercation. Lifting her head to look across, Nicole felt her heart plummet like a stone as her eyes met those of the man being restrained by two of the male staff.

'Just tell them who I am, will you?' Scott demanded.

CHAPTER NINE

TWELVE whole months ago! Nicole stirred herself to move away from the window, with its view across the courtyard to Marcos's apartments, reluctant to relive that dreadful evening. She was supposedly here for a week this time too, but it was going to be hard lasting out that long. If she got really desperate, a phone call to the agency would bring a message summoning her home on some urgent business.

For now, it was essential that she be in complete control of at least her physical responses where Marcos was concerned. Or appear so, at any rate. While it was unlikely that he'd seek any one-to-one encounters, it was best to be prepared for the chance of it happening. The last thing she would want was for him to guess her true state of mind.

Wearing an ankle-length black dress in fluid silk jersey, she went down to the *salón* geared for a tough evening. It was a relief, albeit a temporary one, to find Eduardo alone. Leonora, he said, was still deciding what to put on.

'I'm glad to have this opportunity to speak with you privately,' he admitted when she was seated with a drink to hand. 'I want you to know that any animosity I myself might have felt towards you in the beginning was of short duration. What you did was reprehensible, but I believe your feelings for my son were genuine.'

'They were,' Nicole confirmed huskily as he paused in obvious expectation of an answer from her. 'I never expected to fall in love with him—much less to have him feel the same way for me.' Green eyes directed him a level gaze. 'I know it's hard to believe, but I was already on the verge of breaking things off with Scott when I arrived, because I didn't think I felt enough for him. After meeting your son, I *knew* I didn't. I really did intend telling him the truth. I just kept putting it off for fear of losing him.'

Eduardo inclined his head in tacit acceptance. 'Leonora was at fault too, for allowing us to assume that you were without ties.' He gave a faint sigh. 'I'm afraid she and Marcos will never come to terms with one another.'

The pause stretched. Nicole raked her mind for something else to say, but nothing was forthcoming. It was left to Eduardo to break the silence, tone diffident now.

'I understand you received promotion at your place of work?'

'To manager,' she confirmed.

'There is no man in your life?'

Nicole shook her head. 'I think I'm better off concentrating on my job.'

'But not for always, surely?'

She gave a shrug. 'Who knows?'

'I would hesitate to leave it too long,' said Marcos from the open doorway. 'Even looks such as yours don't last for ever.'

'At twenty-five, I don't think I need start thinking about face-lifts for a while,' Nicole responded, battening down the hatches. 'I realise I'm the last person you'd have wanted to see again, but I'm afraid you'll just have to make the best of it.'

'I intend to,' he said silkily. 'Rest assured of that.'

He advanced into the room, body supple as ever in the black trousers and shirt, the latter open on the brown column of his throat. Nicole swallowed painfully, unable to sustain the cool front in face of the memories coming thick and fast as he moved across her line of vision to the drinks cabinet. She had seen that superb physique stripped of all clothing, had explored every inch with fingers and lips. The hunger rose in her undiluted. It had been so long, so very long!

He took a seat directly opposite, crossing one long leg over the other in a manner that drew the material of his trousers taut across his loins. A quite deliberate provocation, she was sure. He was astute enough to see through any camouflage.

'So, you're here for the christening,' he said, making no effort to mask his scepticism. 'A long way to come for an event in which you play no major part.'

'Nicole is here only after much persuasion,' said Eduardo. 'As Leonora's only surviving family, she—'

'With no blood tie, the relationship can hardly be classed as family,' interposed his son.

'It's the way Leonora sees it,' Nicole declared, hanging onto her outer composure by the skin of her teeth. 'I've no doubt she even looks on you as family, regardless of how you might feel about her.'

'My feelings are of little account,' came the smooth return. 'So, how did you find your new stepbrother?'

I looked in the crib, and there he was; she only just kept the sarcasm at bay. 'He's very handsome,' she said instead. 'Like his father.' She turned a smile in the older man's direction. 'You must be very proud.'

Eduardo returned the smile. 'My only regret is that I will be an old man by the time he reaches maturity.'

'Only if you let yourself be. There are two pensioners, both in their seventies, who live close by my home. One of them appears old because he obviously thinks of himself as old, the other considers himself still in the prime of life, and looks it.'

The smile broadened. 'I must make sure to heed the second example and not the first.'

Marcos made no comment, though the curl of his lip spoke volumes. Nicole refused to let his opinion bother her. The story was true enough, even if she had neglected to mention that the first man suffered from an arthritic condition the other was joyfully free of. Eduardo had taken it the way it was meant, anyway.

She was glad to see Leonora appear in the doorway, looking wonderful as always in shadow-striped silk. Her figure certainly didn't appear to have suffered a great deal.

'Having fun, children?' she asked, looking from one to the other of the younger element in the room. 'My usual, please, darling,' she added to her husband as she moved to take a seat. 'Make it a double, will you? I feel in need of a pick-me-up after spending an hour feeding Luis. Bottle,' she clarified, catching Nicole's eye, 'not breast. I'm willing to go along with a once-a-day bonding session, but that's as *au naturale* as I get!'

'A somewhat selfish attitude, considering the value to the child of the natural method,' commented Marcos, lighting a derisive spark in the blue eyes.

'What would *you* know about it?'

Broad shoulders lifted. 'No degree in child-rearing is needed to be aware that babies fed their mother's milk from birth gain in every way over those deprived of it. It's a long-established fact.'

He was doing this purposely too, Nicole judged,

watching the line of his mouth. Needling his stepmother was obviously a well-established game with
him—one she would have thought Leonora had the
sense not to rise to by now.

Eduardo looked resigned, the lack of cordiality between his wife and son too commonplace to be remarked upon. If Marcos still felt so strongly against his
father's choice of a wife, he should leave them to it
and find a home of his own, thought Nicole. Why
should Leonora have to put up with his disparagement?

She glanced across at him, steeling herself not to
look away again immediately as she met the sardonic
gaze. What she couldn't control was the flush that suf-
fused her face as he ran his eyes slowly over the ex-
panse of smooth, creamy flesh revealed by the wide
scooped neckline of her dress, lingering on the hint of
cleavage for seconds that seemed like minutes.

She could feel her nipples peaking, rubbing painfully
against the lace of her brassière, her skin tingling as if
his hands were caressing her in reality, not just in her
mind. He knew how he made her feel; he couldn't fail
to know. Given half a chance, he might even take advantage of that knowledge, but he wasn't going to get
any chance.

'Shall we be seeing Patricio before the christening?'
she asked with surprising steadiness. 'Isabella too, of
course.'

'They are to join us for luncheon tomorrow,'
Eduardo confirmed. 'Isabella prefers to spend her eve-
nings quietly now that she comes close to term.'

'Another honeymoon baby,' said Leonora drily.
'Though perhaps more of an intention than an accident,
as in our case.'

Having seen the way she had looked at and touched

the child upstairs, Nicole wished she would stop playing that angle. It was hardly likely to improve Marcos's opinion of her, and must cause Eduardo some inner discomfiture.

'A blessing either way,' she stated on a light note. 'I'm looking forward to meeting Luis properly when he's awake. Whose eye colour did he inherit?'

'They were blue to begin with, but very soon darkened,' Leonora confirmed. 'A Peraza through and through!'

'He has his mother's temper,' said Eduardo smilingly. 'Even at twelve weeks, he must have his own way.'

'As if I always have mine!' exclaimed his wife in mock indignation.

'As if I could ever refuse you anything,' he countered, laughing now.

This time Nicole had the sense not to glance in Marcos's direction. Whatever his views, there was nothing wrong with *this* marriage.

He made no further contribution to the conversation, just sat there watching her like some dark avenger. If he *was* brewing ideas of seeking redress, he could forget it, Nicole told herself, knowing even as she thought it that resistance would be hard come by if he did make the attempt. She wanted him now as much as she had ever done. More so, in fact. The deprivation she'd suffered this last year had been hell. Not just sexually, but in every sense. It had been a mistake to come back. One she was probably going to finish up paying for in spades!

Pleading tiredness from the journey, she made her escape soon after dinner. Finding the key missing from her bedroom door lock gave her pause for a moment, but she dismissed the idea that Marcos might have taken it with a view to paying her a visit this very night.

She could even be wrong all the way through about his desire for redress, she thought while preparing for bed. Why would he want to so much as touch her when it was obvious that the very sight of her was anathema to him. He might taunt her with the implied threat of vengeance, but that would be as far as it went.

It was left to Patricio to show any real pleasure on seeing her again. Isabella merely paid lip-service. Apart from the eight-month-old bump concealed beneath her loose gown, she looked very little different from when Nicole had last seen her.

She found herself watching for any sign of the former idolisation in the dark eyes when they rested on Marcos during lunch, but found nothing to create suspicion that the girl still harboured the same feelings for her brother-in-law. She was glad for Patricio's sake. He so obviously worshipped the ground his wife walked upon.

If she hadn't made such an unholy mess of her life, she might have been sitting here in anticipation of a happy event herself, she thought ruefully. She stole a glance in Marcos's direction, heart turning over at the sheer impact of that carved profile. She would have so dearly loved to have had his child.

As if sensing her eyes on him, he looked across, expression hardening. Nicole dropped her gaze, reluctant to have him see her hunger. Whatever the emotions she had aroused in him a year ago, all that existed now was contempt. Hardly surprising, but still agonisingly painful.

He went off somewhere immediately after the meal. Declining to seek the solitude of her bedroom for the siesta hour, Nicole settled herself with a book on one of the loungers. It had been about this same time that Marcos had come to settle scores with her that first day, she recalled achingly, making no sense of the words. She had already fallen for him hook, line and sinker by then, although she had hesitated to acknowledge it. If it hadn't been for Scott…

The fault had been hers, not his, of course. None of it had been his fault. Anyway, there was nothing to be gained from dwelling on the if onlys. She would get through these next few days as best she could, then put it all behind her. No two loves were ever the same, Eduardo had said once. Someone else would come along eventually.

'I hoped to find you alone,' said Patricio, coming into her line of vision from the direction of the house. He dropped to a seat on the edge of the lounger, renewing the memories Nicole had only just put from her mind. 'Isabella still finds it difficult to forgive your trespasses, I'm afraid,' he acknowledged apologetically. 'So I must take the opportunity while she sleeps.'

He paused, viewing her with eyes far more perceptive than they had ever been in the past. 'You still feel for Marcos, don't you?'

It was more of a statement than a question. Nicole briefly contemplated denying it, but couldn't summon the will. 'Do I make it so apparent?' she asked heavily.

'To me, yes. I spent so many years in yearning for Isabella, I feel an affinity with others so burdened. What you did in allowing Marcos to believe you free was very wrong, but I will never be persuaded that you were motivated by the financial advantages alone.'

Nicole made a wry gesture. 'It's what he believes that counts, though, isn't it? Not that I'm not grateful for the vote of confidence—especially when your wife doesn't share your faith.'

'To be joined in matrimony is not to lose one's individuality,' he said. 'I love Isabella with all my heart, but we are each of us entitled to our separate opinions. And before you ask the question,' he went on, proving himself even more perceptive than she had credited, 'she fully realises the difference now between infatuation and true love. We are very happy together.'

'I'm so glad.' Nicole could say it in all sincerity.

'I owe a great deal to you,' he returned. 'Without your urging I might never have found the courage to fight for her attention. You know, of course, that Elena is also married now.'

Nicole inclined her head. 'I heard.'

'The news gave you no fresh hope?'

'Why would it?' she asked. 'I already knew Marcos had no intention of marrying her himself.' She hesitated before putting the question, not even sure she really wanted to know. 'I dare say he has someone lined up by now.'

'There has been no woman in his life this past year,' Patricio replied. 'That much I can state as fact. It must tell you something.'

Nicole searched the striking features so like his older brother's, keeping a tight hold on herself. 'It tells me that he's yet to find a woman he considers worthy of any long-term interest, but I refuse to believe he's gone twelve months without any kind of female contact.'

The shrug was brief. 'About that I can't be so certain, although I find it extremely doubtful that he would stoop to frequenting bordellos in search of physical easement.'

'I didn't mean…' Nicole began, allowing the protest

to fade away in the shamed knowledge that she had meant exactly that. 'I was just being bitchy,' she admitted. 'I'm sure he wouldn't.' She leaned forward on sudden impulse to kiss him lightly on the cheek. 'Thanks, anyway, brother-that-might-have-been. It means a lot to have *your* forgiveness at least.'

Patricio took her hand, lifting it to his lips. 'I wasn't the one hurt. Perhaps if you spoke with Marcos you might convince him of the way you truly feel for him.'

Tone brittle, she said, 'You know your brother. Do you really see him taking my word for anything now? I'm here for the christening. Only the christening. Once that's over, I'm gone for good.'

'You won't return even for *my* son's baptism?'

Nicole had to smile. 'Supposing he turns out to be a she?'

'We are already assured of the baby's sex,' he said, 'and you didn't give me an answer.'

She sighed. 'No, I won't be coming back again. I'd appreciate a photograph, though.'

Patricio looked resigned. 'You shall have it, I promise.' This time it was he who leant forward to place a light kiss on the cheek. 'I'll never forget you, sister-who-almost-was!'

Nicole blinked hard on the moisture in her eyes as he went back indoors. This was almost certainly the last time she would see him on his own. Once the christening was over—if she even made it that far—it would be goodbye to them all. She'd keep in touch with Leonora via letter or phone, of course, but no more visits ever.

The book she was supposed to have been reading had fallen to the floor. She leaned over to pick it up, freezing in the act as she caught sight of the man approaching from the top end of the courtyard. He was wearing riding gear, though whether returning from a ride or just about to set out there was no way of knowing. What wasn't in doubt was the grimness of expression on the chiselled features.

Nicole straightened slowly, pulses leaping all over the place. It was evident that he was making directly for her; evident also that he was good and angry over something. She thought of getting to her feet, in order to meet him on a less disadvantaged level, but her legs refused to move fast enough.

'Have you no shame at all?' he spat out on reaching her. 'Must you prove your continuing attraction even while my brother's wife lies mere yards away with his child in her womb! Don't deny it!' he clipped as she opened her mouth. 'I saw the two of you just now.'

'Saw what exactly?' Nicole managed with fair calm.

Marcos had come to a stop less than a foot away from where she reclined, towering over her. His shirt was open down to the waist, as if to admit the passage of a cooling breeze, the dark hair revealed glistening with moisture. Nicole touched the tip of her tongue to lips gone dry, wondering what he would do if she gave way to the sudden wild urge and flung herself at him to bury her face in the damp thicket. She could almost taste the salty tang.

'You kissed him,' he accused. '*And* incited him into returning the embrace.'

'Hardly an embrace.' Nicole could only wonder at the steadiness of her voice. 'I kissed him on the cheek; he did the same to me. A simple token of friendship, that's all. I realise you're unlikely to look favourably on any kind of amity between us, but I'm not going to spit in his face because of it.'

The dark eyes blazed in sudden ungovernable fury. Bending a knee for support on the lounger edge, he grasped the front of her sleeveless blouse to jerk her upright into reach of his plundering, ruthless mouth. Head pressed back, neck feeling on the verge of breaking, Nicole was helpless to do anything other than pummel with clenched fists at any part of the lean body she could reach, making no impression whatsoever.

Eyes deep jade pools, her breath laboured, she fought to subdue the emotional turmoil when he finally let her go.

'I suppose I had that coming at some point,' she got out.

'You owe me more than a kiss or two,' Marcos gritted. 'If you stay, you'll pay the full price, I promise you!'

'If I go now, I'll miss the christening,' she said unsteadily. 'Would you want me to spit in your father's face too?' She made a small appealing gesture. 'Can't we at least be civilised about it for his sake?'

A muscle clenched along his jawline as he regarded the captivating face upturned to his. 'Why should I treat a woman such as yourself with any respect at all? Like your stepmother, your interests are purely self-motivated.'

'You might have thought that about Leonora once,' Nicole disputed, leaving the slur on her own character aside for the moment, 'but you'd have to be blind not to see how she feels about your father. She's had his child, for heaven's sake!'

'An accident, she claims.' He was standing upright again, hands driven deep into his breeches pockets, face hard as iron. 'An insurance against any possible change of heart on my father's part, I would say. She hated every moment of her pregnancy. Neither has she any real feeling for the child.'

It was probably true, Nicole reflected, about her hating the months of physical and hormonal changes; just losing her figure would have been enough to send her into depression. It was quite definitely true that she had little interest in playing full-time mother, but there had been no doubting the tenderness in the blue eyes when she had held her son in her arms this morning.

'Not all women are born with the mothering instinct,' she said, 'but that doesn't mean they don't care. As to getting pregnant as an insurance. No way! It would never have occurred to Leonora that she might ever have need. The trouble with you, Marcos,' she continued, gathering her resources, 'is that you're not prepared to make any concessions whatsoever once you've set your mind. All right, I treated you badly. I know it would be a waste of time and effort trying to convince you that my feelings for you were genuine, and I don't expect you to either forgive or forget, but we can surely put it all aside for the few days I'm going to be here? You'll never see me again after that.'

Something flickered briefly in the dark eyes, but there was no yielding of expression. 'As you say, I make no concessions,' he stated flatly.

Nicole sank back slowly into the padded cushion as he stalked off. The threat hadn't been an idle one, for certain. If she stayed, she paid.

So do it, she thought recklessly. She could at least have that much of him—perhaps even stand a chance of getting through to him. He'd loved her once. Who was to say that love couldn't be revived? Even if it wasn't, what did she have to lose outside of a little false pride?

She went up to the nursery at five, and spent half an hour playing with the wide-awake baby under Juanita's watchful eye. He was an absolute delight, gurgling with laughter when she tickled him, and looking as if he understood every word she said. Only when deprived of the finger knuckle he was kneading between his gums did he show signs of the temper Eduardo had spoken of, sticking out a mutinous lip and letting out a bellow loud enough to shatter eardrums.

'Strong lungs,' commented Juanita proudly as Nicole hastily complied with his demand. 'He will grow up to be a strong man.

'You should have a baby of your own,' she added. 'You would make a good mother.'

Although the girl hadn't been here a year ago, it was hardly likely that she was unaware of events prior to her arrival, Nicole reckoned, but there was nothing in her manner to suggest the hostility evident in some members of staff.

'I hope to some day,' she acknowledged. 'Several of them, in fact.' She gave an exclamation as Luis fastened gleeful fingers into her hair. 'Ouch, you little horror! That hurts!'

Laughing, Juanita came to help her disentangle herself, eliciting further protesting yowls from Luis. They were still battling to uncurl the clutching fingers without hurting him when Marcos walked into the room.

'If you can't keep that child quiet—' he began, breaking off abruptly as he took in the little tableau. 'What the devil…?'

'No devil, just your little brother exercising his Peraza tenacity of purpose,' Nicole retorted in English. 'Sorry if you were disturbed, but it's what babies tend to do at this age.'

'And you would know so much about babies, of course,' he said with irony.

Framed in the doorway, clad now in close-fitting cream trousers and tan silk shirt, his hair looking as if he had just run frustrated fingers through it, he made her yearn. It took everything she had to keep her voice from betraying her.

'Rather more than you would, for certain. It's called natural instinct—helped along, I admit, by experience with a friend who has one.' Nicole handed the still complaining child over to the hovering Juanita, giving her a reassuring smile. 'I'll leave you to settle him down.'

Marcos stood back from the door to allow her exit from the room; the anger had given way to something less easily defined. 'Who are you attempting to impress with your maternal instincts?' he asked.

'Obviously not you,' she said. 'I could hardly be sure a few cries would fetch you along.'

'A few!' For the first time a shadow of the man she had known a year ago showed through in the wry smile. 'I'm woken every single night!'

'Perhaps you should think about getting a place of your own,' Nicole ventured. 'I know Las Veridas has been the family home for a long time, but—'

'As it will be for a long time more,' he declared with a swift return to animosity. 'Leonora has dominion only while my father lives.'

'I'd doubt very much whether she'd want to stay on here without him, anyway.' Nicole was sure she was right about that. 'The *casa* has never held all that much attraction for her. It's too old and dark for her tastes.'

'I'm aware of it,' he said. 'She's tried to introduce

changes. Fortunately there are limits to even my father's indulgence.'

'Well, then?' She was pushing it, Nicole knew, but some inner devil drove her on. 'It's obviously safe enough in his hands, so why not leave him to it for his lifetime? You'd be far better off in one of those luxury apartment blocks downtown. There'd be no crying babies around to disturb your sleep in that kind of environment, I'd bet. Ideal for bachelor pursuits, though. In fact—'

She broke off as he seized hold of her, giving vent to a yelp at the sudden hard contact with the wall at her back. Marcos held her pinned there, his mouth a thin, taut line. 'I'll take no more of your effrontery!' he ground out. 'One more word from you, and I'll treat you the way you deserve to be treated.'

Nicole held her tongue. There was a line to be drawn and she'd reached it. Her eyes were on a level with the open collar of his shirt; she wanted so badly to put her lips to the hollow of his throat, to plead with him for a second chance.

Her throat constricted as he relaxed his grasp on one shoulder and moved the hand downwards to reach the curve of her breast, but there was no brutality in the touch of the long, lean fingers. She closed her eyes, savouring the sensation, willing him not to stop. He had to have some feeling left for her to caress her with such exquisite sensitivity; he *had* to!

The deprivation when he removed his hand was exquisite in quite another sense. She opened her eyes with reluctance, to meet the sardonic regard and realise just how futile her hope of reconciliation was.

'I look forward to further recompense,' he said. 'And soon.'

Nicole found her voice with an effort. 'As you said, I owe you.'

The sarcasm increased. 'If you think to deter me from claiming that debt by passivity, you can, as you would say, think again. I intend to extract full satisfaction.'

He released her, inclining his head in a mocking bow. 'Until then, *chica*!'

CHAPTER TEN

DESPITE her lengthy afternoon rest, Isabella looked tired when she and Patricio left at six. Eight months of pregnancy were enough to drain anyone of energy, said Leonora, when Nicole commented on the younger girl's lack of vivacity.

'At her age, she'll soon bounce back once the baby's here,' she declared. 'It took me a good month to start feeling myself again—especially round the waistline!'

'You'd never know there'd been any difference,' Nicole assured her.

'Considering the effort I put into regaining lost ground, I'd certainly hope not,' the other returned drily. 'Anyway, what did you do with yourself this afternoon?'

Nicole kept her tone easy. 'Oh, just lazed around. I looked in on Luis for half an hour or so. He's such a live wire! I thought I might take him for an airing round the grounds in the morning, if that's all right?'

'I can't think why not. Juanita would probably welcome the break.' Leonora eyed her curiously. 'You really would love one of your own, wouldn't you?'

Not just *any* one, Nicole could have told her. Her smile was forced. 'Some day, maybe.'

Eduardo's return from seeing off his son and daughter-in-law was a welcome reprieve from any further discussion along those lines. It wasn't a subject she cared to pursue.

Marcos didn't put in an appearance for dinner. As

neither Eduardo nor Leonora made any reference to his absence, Nicole could only assume that they'd known he wouldn't be dining at home tonight.

Trying to persuade herself that it was a relief not to have him in her sights every time she lifted her eyes from the table proved a waste of time and effort. Wherever he was, he wouldn't be alone, for certain. The thought of him with some other woman was sheer torment.

The storm that broke around eleven was unusual for the time of year. A sign of the increasingly erratic weather patterns worldwide, Eduardo observed.

'Marcos will do well to remain where he is for the night,' he said, watching the rain beating down in the courtyard.

'Where might that be?' asked Leonora casually.

'The city,' he answered.

'Pleasure or business?'

'Business.' He turned away from the window to resume his seat, his glance resting a brief moment on Nicole. 'All business.'

She didn't believe it. She was pretty sure *he* didn't believe it either. For what difference it made.

It was sunshine as usual in the morning. Tired of trousers, Nicole put on a short cotton sundress in bright yellow, teaming it with a matching scarf to tie back her hair.

'You bring a ray of sunlight with you,' declared Eduardo approvingly when she joined him for breakfast.

He was alone. As Leonora had failed to put in an appearance until gone ten yesterday morning, Nicole hadn't expected to see her, but against all the odds she had harboured a faint hope that Marcos would have made it back last night after all.

'Marcos will have stayed at the apartment in town,' advised Eduardo, as if guessing her thoughts.

'I didn't realise he had an apartment in town,' she said after a moment.'

'But of course. For many years. Patricio too, until he married.'

'Somewhere private to take women-friends, I suppose.'

'Perhaps so, on occasion,' he returned mildly. 'You believe it was such an occasion last night?'

Nicole bit her lip. 'It's really no concern of mine whether it was or wasn't.'

'Marcos was entertaining some foreign business associates who wished to sample the city nightlife,' Eduardo continued, as though she hadn't spoken. 'His return was doubtful, even without the storm.'

Especially with nothing to bring him back in a hurry, she reflected. She was here for several more days; he could afford to bide his time, to keep her wondering when and where he would strike—or even if.

'As I said,' she intoned, 'it's really no business of mine. Did you see Luis yet this morning?'

Eduardo accepted the change of subject with a smile. 'Of course. I visit him morning, noon and evening. It's still a source of wonderment to me that I have another child. And of a certain concern that I may not see him grow to maturity,' he added on a more sober note.

'You're only in your mid-fifties now,' said Nicole, forgetting her own troubles for the moment. 'And there doesn't seem much wrong with your health. Barring accidents, you've every chance of making it to a hundred.'

Eduardo pulled a comical face. 'I'm not at all sure I would want to live *quite* that long!'

Recalling the voiced concern when wheeling the Rolls Royce of a pram through the landscaped gardens later, Nicole was torn by the knowledge that she almost certainly wouldn't see Luis grow to maturity. She wondered what kind of man the mixture of genes in his blood would make. A strong-minded one, for certain.

'Handsome too,' she told him, raising a chuckle. 'You'll have all the girls crazy for you!'

She continued to talk to the child as they traversed the negotiable paths. Apart from a couple of men tending the prolific plant life, they had the gardens to themselves. Superbly sprung though the pram undoubtedly was, its size and weight proved cumbersome at times. Luis would be just as comfortable, and far less enclosed, in one of the lightweight buggies favoured by most parents these days, Nicole considered, glad to stop for a few minutes' rest on a stone bench strategically placed at the top of the incline she had just ascended.

The view from where she sat was tremendous, looking out across the driveway some feet below to the mountains ringing the valley. On impulse, she got up to take Luis from the pram, holding him securely in her arms to show him the scene.

'Behold the family seat!'

Judging from the sudden look of concentration on the small face, Luis had his mind on rather more pressing matters right now. A good thing she'd brought a spare nappy along with her, Nicole reflected, wrinkling her nose. Babies would be babies, however highborn they might be.

She turned to deposit him back in the pram in order

to change him, halting in horrified disbelief on seeing it teetering on the very edge of the slope down to the drive. It went over before she could move—not that she could have done much with Luis in her arms—bouncing high in the air as it hit a partly exposed tree root and coming down again with a crash onto the drive itself just as a car came round the bend from the road.

The screech of brakes forcefully applied set Nicole's teeth on edge. Had Marcos been travelling any faster, he wouldn't have been able to avoid crushing the pram beneath the Lamborghini wheels. As it was, the vehicle finished up slewed halfway across the drive with the bonnet mere inches from a tree trunk.

Frozen to the spot, Nicole watched him thrust open the door and get out of the car. She braced herself as he lifted a scorching gaze to where she stood, having first ascertained that the pram was empty.

'*Imbécil!*' he ejaculated. 'Do you not even have the sense to apply a brake!'

'I did!' she said, recovering sufficient command of herself to resent the imprecation, even while still shaking at the thought of what might have happened.

'Then how do you explain *this*?' He indicated the now far from pristine baby carriage. 'It's only by good fortune that the child wasn't inside!'

'Do you think I don't know that?' Nicole demanded fiercely. 'The brake must be faulty.'

Alarmed by the angry voices, Luis let out a wail. She hugged him closer, speaking softly, soothingly, trying not to dwell on the might have beens. There was no doubt in her mind about that brake. She clearly remembered shifting the lever over when she stopped to take a breather.

The question was, had she shifted it far enough for

it not to spring back when she lifted Luis out? Legs suddenly weak, she regained her seat on the bench, heart dropping like a stone as she watched Marcos testing the brake, with no evidence of failure. The fault was hers. It had to be.

The set expression on the hard-hewn features seemed to waver momentarily when he looked up at her, but it must have been a trick of the light because there was nothing soft about his voice when he said, 'Wait there.'

He parked the damaged pram on one side of the drive, then got back into the car, straightening it up to head for the *casa* around the next bend. It would take him several minutes to reach her on foot via the path, Nicole calculated. She was quite capable of carrying Luis that far, but she obviously wasn't to be trusted to do it without further incident. Marcos could do the carrying himself.

He came alone, striding up the path as if in a hurry to reach her before anything else happened. It was the first time she had seen him in jeans; the taut fit about lean hips did nothing for her equilibrium.

She got to her feet as he reached her, placing the child in the arms he raised in instinctive response to her purposeful movement. Luis returned his brother's somewhat nonplussed regard unblinkingly, then let go with a resounding raspberry. For a brief moment the dark eyes lit with involuntary amusement, altering expression abruptly as the odour hit home.

'One of the other things babies tend to do,' advised Nicole woodenly. 'I'd suggest you take him straight up to Juanita, while I go on ahead and let your father and Leonora know what happened.'

She forced herself to maintain a steady pace on the way, refusing to look back to see how he was coping with the now loudly protesting baby. However distasteful a burden he might find the child, he'd keep him safe enough.

Finding Leonora and Eduardo together helped a little. She gave them the bare facts, making no attempt to downplay her negligence.

'Luis is unhurt. That is the most important thing,' Eduardo assured her kindly. 'The carriage can be easily replaced.'

Belying her sometimes careless approach to motherhood, Leonora had already departed to check on the child. Nicole hesitated before making the suggestion. 'Please don't think I'm trying to make any excuses, but something a little smaller and lighter might not be a bad idea. Juanita would certainly find it easier to manage when she takes him for an airing.'

'It shall be done,' he promised. 'The other was—' He broke off, shaking his head. 'No matter.'

Nicole had a very good idea of what he had been going to say. Leonora would have insisted on having top of the range in everything, regardless of suitability. Not that that was any excuse either.

'You say Marcos insisted on carrying Luis back to the house himself?' Eduardo queried.

'That's right.' Not for anything would Nicole have robbed him of the hope that his older son was showing signs of sibling attachment at last. 'I suppose he'll arrange for someone to fetch the pram off the drive.'

'Already done,' said the he in question, coming out from the house in time to catch the last words. 'I've arranged for it to be taken away by the company representative, who will be bringing a selection of possible replacements later today.'

Eduardo looked gratified. 'That was thoughtful of you. Is Leonora still with Luis?'

'As far as I know.'

'Then I will go and join her.'

Nicole kept her eyes fixed on the glass containing the brandy Eduardo had insisted on having fetched to calm her nerves. Marcos made no move to sit down.

'Juanita tells me that the brake pedal is very stiff and requires extra force to move it all the way over,' he said. 'She blames herself for not pointing this out to you.'

This time Nicole did look up, though only as far as his chest, registering the fresh white shirt; Luis had obviously made his presence felt in more ways than one. 'It isn't her fault. I should have been more careful. You were right to call me an imbecile. Luis could have been killed.'

'I've called you far worse at times,' he stated. 'In my mind, if not the words themselves.'

Nicole swallowed hard. 'I can imagine.'

'I would doubt that. You can have no concept of what I felt on discovering your duplicity.' He drew a harsh breath. 'You were clever; I'll grant you that. You employed exactly the right tactics to lull me into believing you innocent of any ulterior motive.'

'It wasn't like that. I really did—' She broke off, shaking her head. 'You're as unlikely to believe the truth now as you were then.'

'That you had already decided to end your engagement before we met? That you'd never known what love really was until you found it with me? That you intended telling me about your fiancé before we departed for your homeland?' The derision seared.

'Would you have even considered doing so if I hadn't insisted on accompanying you?'

Would she? Nicole couldn't honestly swear to it. 'Possibly not,' she admitted. 'I was so afraid of losing you.'

'Along with everything else you stood to gain.'

'I didn't give a damn about all this!' Her head was up now, her eyes shooting green flames. 'It was you I was in love with! I could hardly believe it when you asked me to marry you.'

The muscles along his jawline were taut as bow-strings, his whole face a granite mask. 'The result of allowing a beautiful face and body to sway my judgement.'

'If looks were all it took, how come Elena failed to get you to propose to *her*?' she flashed back, refusing to believe that lust had been the governing emotion.

'Elena didn't provide the same incentive.'

'You mean she wouldn't sleep with you first!'

'I mean,' he said, 'that she failed to stir me into even wanting her to sleep with me. No fault of hers.' His mouth twisted. 'You were aware of what *you* made me feel the moment we met. I saw it in your eyes.'

'All I saw in yours was hostility. The same thing I'm seeing now.' Nicole lifted her shoulders in a re-signed gesture. 'This whole conversation is a waste of breath. Nothing I can say is going to convince you that my feelings are genuine.'

'Are?' The tone was cynical.

It had been a slip of the tongue, but Nicole was past caring. 'Yes, *are*,' she said flatly. 'If you want the truth, I've spent the last twelve months hoping against hope that things could somehow be put right again between us. I realise now how hopeless it is.'

Marcos regarded her in silence for a lengthy moment, his expression undergoing an indefinable alteration. 'I've heard it said that actions speak louder than words. If you really feel the way you say, then prove it to me.'

Heart jerking, she said huskily, 'How?'

'By coming to me tonight. Unconditionally.'

Voluntary surrender with no assurance that it would make any difference to the ultimate outcome. That was what he was asking. Nicole gazed at him with darkened eyes, finding no chink in the armour.

'A test of my feelings,' she said, 'or just payback?'

He gave a brief shrug. 'A risk you take.'

Nicole reached for the brandy glass as he moved away, tossing back the contents in a single swallow. The spirit spread warmth through her chest. She was going to take that risk, she already knew. She couldn't *not* take it.

Leonora offered no word of reproof on her return from the nursery. She was only too relieved, she said, that all had ended well.

'I suppose I should thank Marcos for actually carrying Luis back to the house,' she added with reluctance. A faint smile crossed her face. 'Especially with a full nappy! Poetic justice, some might call it. He hasn't exactly smothered *me* in roses.'

'He was coming round until I messed everything up,' said Nicole wryly. 'You've borne the brunt the last twelve months.'

'Nothing I can't handle,' the other assured her. 'In fact, I find crossing swords with him quite stimulating at times. One thing I'll grant him: he puts on a good face for outsiders, so we'll neither of us be running any gauntlets tonight.'

Nicole felt her heart drop. 'Tonight?'

'Dinner with the godparents, and one or two more. Informal, so wear what you feel comfortable in.'

What she would feel most comfortable in was her room, Nicole reflected, hating the thought of facing people who would all have been witness to that scene at the wedding. Embarrassing not just for her but surely for Marcos too. The only way to handle it would be to act as if nothing untoward had ever happened, but it wouldn't be easy.

It wasn't, but she coped, schooling herself to turn a blind eye to the glances, a deaf ear to the occasional overheard remark. Although he must be aware of the speculation, Marcos gave no sign of discomfiture, even on finding her placed next to him at dinner; an attempt on Leonora's part to make them spend at least an hour or two in close proximity, Nicole assumed. She wondered what her former stepmother would think of her plans for even closer proximity later.

With no more than ten at table, conversation was fairly general. Mostly in English too, as Leonora's Spanish hadn't progressed beyond a few basic phrases. Why go to the trouble of learning the language when almost everyone spoke English? she'd said in answer to Nicole's mild comment.

Nicole made little contribution herself, too vitally aware of the man at her side to pay much attention to what was being said. Remembering the way it felt to be held close in his arms, to be kissed and caressed until her whole body was on fire, to have that potent weight pressuring her thighs apart, his hands sliding beneath her, lifting her to take him. At the very least she would have that much of him again.

The evening seemed to go on for ever. Reaching her room at long last, she took a shower and smoothed delicately perfumed cream over her skin before putting on a black satin nightdress and matching negligee. The green eyes looking back at her through the mirror as she brushed her hair into a shining cascade were far from serene, but there was no thought in her mind of backing out.

The house was quiet when she finally left her room. Feet clad in brief black mules, she silently traversed the corridor to the far side of the courtyard, hesitating for a heart-thudding moment or two outside Marcos's bedroom, wondering a little ridiculously whether to knock or simply go on in.

She chose the latter in the end, coming to a stop just inside the door on seeing him stretched out naked on top of the bedcovers, his body lit by the glow from the two bedside lamps. He was dormant; that much she could ascertain from where she stood. It was going to be up to her, she assumed, to alter that state of affairs. She touched her tongue to lips turned dry as old parchment, unable to come up with a solitary word.

'Close the door,' he said.

Nicole did so, finding her voice with an effort. 'You were so sure I was going to come?'

'Sure enough.' The smile that curved his lips as he scrutinised her was not of the humorous variety. 'You look very beautiful. But you know that, of course.' He put up a hand as she started to speak. 'No more words. Take off your negligee.'

He was going to make her undress right there in front of him, Nicole guessed. Humiliating only if she allowed it to be. She unfastened the tiny buttons holding the front of the garment together, sliding it from her shoulders and allowing it to fall to the floor, then following it with the nightdress. She saw his jaw contract as he studied her slenderly curving length—the involuntary stirring of his body.

Carriage proud, she crossed the room without haste, coming to a halt at the bedside. Her skin looked like alabaster in contrast to his, her hair like the rising sun in the lamplight. Marcos drew her down to the bed, looking into her eyes as he splayed his fingers across her fluttering stomach muscles.

'You think by this you will soon have me at your feet again?' he said softly.

'When were you ever at *any* woman's feet?' she rejoined, fighting to stay on top of the flaring desire. 'I'm here because I couldn't stay away. Because I've missed you every waking minute of every day since we parted.'

There was a hint of cruelty in the curl of his lip. 'There are other men who could satisfy your needs.'

'In a purely physical sense, perhaps there are. I wouldn't know. I wouldn't even want to know.' Her voice tremored a little. 'I love you, Marcos. That's the difference. The problem is there's no real way of proving it to you.'

'None,' he agreed. 'If you stay with me tonight it alters nothing.'

It was what she had known all along deep down, thought Nicole hollowly. He'd never had any intention of letting her through the barriers. 'You said *if* I stay,' she managed, still clutching at straws. 'Does that mean I have a choice?'

He shrugged. 'If you wish to leave, by all means go.'

Chest tight as a drum, she lifted a hand to trace the

line of his mouth with a trembling fingertip. 'I can't,' she whispered. 'I want you too much.'

Passion flared suddenly in the dark eyes, the hand spanning her stomach moving up to curve her breast as he lowered his head to find her mouth. The kiss was almost savage in its intensity, her response equally so. She locked her hands behind the dark head to hold him close, thrusting the lower half of her body into contact with his hardness, desperate to have him inside her where he, and only he, belonged. They slid together as if they'd never been apart, moving as one in the mounting frenzy of desire. Nicole was lost to everything but the moment, incapable of controlling the cries torn from her lips as they reached the zenith in perfect unison and went into freefall.

She came back to awareness by slow degrees, the warm weight of the body still joined so closely to hers eliciting a soaring happiness and relief. She put her lips to the head at rest on her shoulder, seeing a reflection of her own inner glow in the dark eyes as he lifted to look down at her. For a few seconds it seemed that everything was going to be all right—that he was ready to forgive and forget. The sudden hardening of his expression carried all the impact of a dash of ice-cold water in the face.

'*This* is all you get from me,' he said through gritted teeth.

Nicole lay like a log as he withdrew from her, mind and body numb. It took every ounce of will-power she had to get her on her feet and across the room to where she had dropped both nightdress and negligee. It would help if she could hate him, but she couldn't. Not yet, at least. A risk she had to take, he'd said this afternoon. Well, she'd taken it. End of story.

There was no sound from him when she left the room. Payment at last extracted, he could rest in peace. She wished him joy of it.

Sleep was a long time coming. It was still two full days to the christening. Nicole didn't think she could stick it out that long. The mistake she'd made was in coming at all. How could she have thought for a moment that Marcos might be prepared to let bygones be bygones? His love had died a year ago. There had never been any chance of resurrection.

She was heavy-eyed in the morning, but resolute. The very first chance she got, she was going to put through a call to her next in command at the agency and arrange for him to call back summoning her home on urgent business. If she couldn't get a direct flight she would take whatever was available—even if it meant changing planes several times. Anything was better than staying on here to face Marcos's relentless hostility.

There was no one in the hall when she went down. With the time back home already creeping up to midday, Nicole took a chance and made the call, thankful to get through without too much delay. Andrew promised to do as she asked within the hour, containing his obvious curiosity.

Going out to join the others at breakfast was one of the hardest things she had ever done, although she needn't have worried because Marcos wasn't there. If he'd gone somewhere for the day, there was a chance she might even get away before he returned. He would probably guess that she'd arranged the summons herself, but that was by the by. Not having to face him again after last night would be a godsend.

The call came through twenty minutes later. Nicole

put on a show of resigned acceptance for the benefit of anyone who did happen to overhear her end of the conversation, keeping it going on her return to tell Leonora and Eduardo the news.

'It's needs must, I'm afraid,' she said, feeling a total heel in face of the latter's obvious disappointment.

Leonora said nothing right then, but her disbelief came through loud and clear. She lost little time in voicing her opinion the moment the two of them were alone.

'Whatever's gone on between you and Marcos, I'd have credited you with enough guts to see it through,' she stated bluntly. 'There's no emergency. You're running away!'

Denials were a waste of time and breath, Nicole knew. She gave a wry shrug. 'So I'm gutless. Anyway, I need to phone the airport.'

'Hopefully all flights are fully booked!' Leonora shot after her.

The hope was almost borne out. The earliest available seat was on a flight via Miami the next day. Nicole took it, resigning herself to spending one more night here. No more pining for what might have been, she thought staunchly. It was time to get on with her life.

Lunch came and went without Marcos putting in an appearance. Apparently he'd taken the plane up early on, leaving no word as to his destination. Unusually irresponsible behaviour, Eduardo declared. Discourteous too.

'I had hoped that matters would be resolved between the two of you,' he told Nicole ruefully. 'But it appears it is not to be. That is no reason for you to feel unable to visit again, however.'

'She won't, though,' said Leonora, directing her a challenging blue gaze. 'Will you?'

Nicole hesitated only a moment before shaking her head. 'I don't think it would be a very good idea.' She made a determined effort to lighten her tone. 'Would you mind if I took a ride?'

'You are welcome to do whatever you wish, providing you take due care,' Eduardo assured her. 'The stable hands will prepare a mount for you.'

Leonora made no further comment. She had, Nicole took it, given up even trying.

The afternoon was drawing towards early evening by the time she reached the stables. She asked to have Rojo saddled, surprised and not a little gratified when the gelding appeared to recognise her scent. She hadn't ridden at all in the last year, so it was going to be necessary to take it easy if she didn't want to spend a very uncomfortable journey home tomorrow. No more than an hour, she promised herself.

She took the same trail Marcos had taken her down that very first morning, pausing to wallow in emotive memories for a moment or two at the spot where he had caught up with her that first day. If she had told him the truth then he would have left her alone, but she hadn't wanted him to leave her alone. What she hadn't anticipated was his falling in love with her too— or at least with the image he'd had of her.

All past and gone now. From here on in she had to look forward, not back. She had her job, her home, an adequate social life; enough to be going on with. Eventually she'd meet someone else she could care for.

She left it to Rojo to choose his own path after that, sitting easily in the saddle, not thinking of anything very much. Apart from the rustling of leaves, the occasional cry of a bird, the forest was remarkably silent.

It took the cooling temperature to remind her that nightfall wasn't all that far away. With no clear idea by then of which way was home, she simply turned Rojo about and gave him his head again, trusting him to retrace his steps. They'd already been out longer than intended, she realised, looking at her watch. It was probably going to be dark by the time they did get back.

A louder rustle from overhead tilted her head upwards in time to catch a glimpse of a wizened little face and furry body. The monkey chattered at her angrily, joined by what sounded like at least four or five more, although they remained unseen in the canopy. Something crashed through the undergrowth off to her right, lifting the hair at the back of her neck despite the fact that whatever it was was obviously too timid to stand its ground.

None of the larger species of cat inhabited the area, she remembered Marcos saying. Neither would Eduardo have countenanced her riding out alone had there been any really dangerous wildlife around. Seated up here, she was safe enough from snakes and such— always providing they didn't drop on her from the trees.

Eyes drawn upwards again in involuntary response to the thought, she was taken totally unawares when Rojo suddenly gave vent to a frantic whinny and reared. The earth came up to meet her with a thump that drove every ounce of breath from her body for a moment. Lying there dazedly, she heard the fast retreating thud of hooves, and knew she really *was* in trouble now.

She pushed herself upright in time to see the tail end of something long and sinuous disappear into the undergrowth on the far side of the trail. Snakes were only dangerous when cornered, she'd heard, but it was little comfort. Her best hope was that Rojo would have calmed down enough to stop further along the trail.

On her feet again, she took a moment or two to settle her nerves before setting off in the wake of her mount. At least she appeared to have escaped the fall with nothing worse than a few bruises, although they were going to prove painful enough in a few hours' time, she knew from past experience.

Silent as the forest had been earlier, it now seemed to teem with sound. Nicole set her teeth against the welling panic when it became obvious that Rojo hadn't stopped. Even if it wasn't the one leading back to the *casa*, the trail she was on had to go somewhere. Providing she kept her eyes peeled for any more snakes, she'd be just fine.

Nightfall brought a whole new perspective. With little moonlight penetrating the green canopy, it was a case of making as much noise as she could in the hope that anything on the trail would hear her coming and get out of the way. She went through every song she could remember, substituting 'la-la' where she didn't know the words. If it did nothing else, it drowned out the rustlings and snufflings that seemed to come from all around.

The relief when she saw a light and heard the shout from up ahead was so overwhelming it took her a moment or two to gather herself to reply. Powerful torchlight turned the encroaching trees from black to green again as a man on horseback rounded the bend ahead, pinning her in its beam.

Dazzled, she threw an arm over her eyes, but she didn't need sight to tell her who her rescuer was. Marcos dismounted, sticking the torch under the saddle flap before striding over to pull her into his arms, his mouth searing in its claim.

'I thought to find you injured, or even worse,' he said roughly, still holding her close. 'Never have I known an agony such as I've suffered this past hour since Rojo returned without you. I was coming to find you, to tell you of my shame for the way I behaved towards you last night. It gave me none of the satisfaction I sought, believe me.'

'It doesn't matter,' Nicole whispered. 'It really doesn't matter.'

'It matters a great deal,' he declared. 'How can a man who would treat the woman he loves with such brutality ever be trusted again?'

'Trust cuts both ways,' she said, still not wholly convinced that this was really happening. 'If you can put faith in me again, then I can surely do it too.'

Left unattended, the stallion performed a restless dance, shifting the torch so that its light struck upwards into the treetops to give rise to a burst of excited monkey chatter. Marcos let Nicole go in order to seize the animal's reins, holding it in check.

'We had better be on our way before he decides to head for home without us,' he said. 'There will be time enough to sort out our affairs when we get there.'

He took what turned out to be a whistle from his pocket and blew three long blasts to tell the others also out searching for her that she had been found. Extracting the torch from under the saddle flap, he helped Nicole mount, then swung himself up behind her and urged the horse into motion.

'Shine it on the ground ahead,' he instructed, passing her the torch to hold.

He rose one-handed, as always, the other secure about her waist. She could feel the warmth of his breath on her nape where the hair had parted, the hard strength of his body at her back. Even now, she found it difficult to credit that things were working out after all.

'You haven't asked me how I came to fall off Rojo,' she said.

'It's sufficient to know that you survived the fall,' he answered softly. 'I would have died a thousand deaths if I'd never been able to tell you what you mean to me.'

'What do I mean to you?' she asked unevenly, and felt his arm tighten about her.

'Everything,' he said. 'I tried this past year to put you from my mind, but you wouldn't be put. Other women have held no interest for me since the moment I set eyes on you. I mistrusted you initially, yes, but you soon overcame my doubts. For the first time I knew what it was to love as well as to want. I'd never seriously contemplated marriage before, but with you I could think of nothing else.'

'Until I destroyed it all by proving your original assessment right,' Nicole said wryly. 'It was true that I'd already decided I'd made a bad mistake in agreeing to marry Scott, but that was no excuse for pretending he didn't even exist. I treated you both abominably.'

Marcos put his lips to her nape in a caress so gentle it started tears in her eyes. 'No worse than I've treated you these last days. I wanted to hurt you the way I was hurting. The way I've never stopped hurting. Making you come to me the way I did was…'

'You didn't make me,' she protested. 'I came of my own free will.'

'Not to be used to satisfy an unholy desire for revenge. You came in the hope that we might begin again, while I had no intention of allowing it. I only came to my senses after you'd gone.'

Nicole nestled her head back against his chest, her cup overflowing. 'Is that why you took off this morning?'

'I couldn't bring myself to face you,' he admitted. 'I planned to stay away until after you left, even though it meant missing the christening. But it proved impossible. I had to return. Finding you missing—' He broke off, the tone enough to indicate his frame of mind at the time. 'I love you, *mi amada*,' he said thickly. 'More than life itself. Will you make your home here with me?'

'I'm already home,' she answered.

EPILOGUE

'YOU'RE NOT disappointed?' Nicole asked a little anxiously.

Marcos shook his head, mouth curving. 'It's said that the most virile men father girls. To make two at the one time proves me a potent force indeed!'

'Through and through,' Nicole confirmed, reassured as much by the humour as the denial. She looked back to the twin bundles in her arms, even now scarcely able to believe they were real. They'd known there were two of them for months, of course, though they'd neither of them wanted to know the sex in advance. 'They're so beautiful!' she breathed.

'Like their mother,' Marcos said softly. 'Their brave, beautiful mother who suffered so greatly to bring them into the world.'

'It wasn't that bad.' She smiled. 'Not with you holding my hand. Anyway, it's worth any amount of pain to have them both safe and sound.'

'You must get some rest,' he said. 'They will be well taken care of while you sleep.'

'I know.' She gave a contented sigh. 'It isn't a dream. They'll still be here when I wake up.'

'So,' he said, 'shall I. Always and for ever, *mi amada.*'

Nicole looked into the dark eyes, secure in the love written so plainly there. 'I can't wait to come home to you.'

'Nor I to have you there again.'

'Home.' She savoured the word. 'It was so wonder-ful of your father to turn Las Veridas over to us.'

'Under pressure from his wife to provide her with a home more suited to her tastes,' came the dry comment. 'He gives way to her far too easily.'

'You can hardly say he looks unhappy on it,' Nicole said mildly, having long ago accepted that the relationship between her husband and former stepmother was never likely to reach great heights. 'Anyway, I'm glad she took Inéz with her. I far prefer keeping house myself—especially now I seem to be back in favour again.'

Marcos smiled. 'You proved yourself a worthy mistress these past months. As a mother, you'll find yourself even more highly regarded. And I know you said you intended taking full care of the children yourself, but I've hired a young woman Juanita recommended to provide some assistance for you. You'll please me by not arguing about it,' he added firmly as she opened her mouth to protest. 'Two babies are too much for one person to handle.'

Nicole gave in, recognising adamancy when she heard it. He was probably right anyway, she conceded. A little help wouldn't go amiss.

The door opened to admit the nurse in charge pushing a cot on wheels. 'I must insist that you rest now,' she said. 'I will take the babies to the nursery.'

Nicole gave the sleeping pair over with reluctance, forced to acknowledge for herself a weariness only sleep could assuage.

'Two more minutes,' the nurse instructed Marcos, with a severity that brought a gleam of amusement to the dark eyes.

'A woman of some command,' he said as she de-

parted. 'But she is right; I must leave you for now.'
He bent to put his lips to Nicole's with a tenderness
more telling than any passion. 'Sleep well, soul of my
soul!' he murmured in Spanish.

Eyes already beginning to close, she watched him
out of the room, this man who held her heart for all
time. He would soon be back.

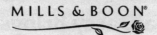

MILLS & BOON®

Makes any time special

Enjoy a romantic novel from
Mills & Boon®

Presents...™   *Enchanted*™   TEMPTATION.

Historical Romance™   ↲MEDICAL ROMANCE™

Emma Darcy brings you...

Meet the Kings, three brothers with three very different lifestyles, all living in the outback of Australia. Join the Kings of the Outback in their search for soulmates.

The Playboy King's Wife

4th August

The Pleasure King's Bride

3rd November

FREE

4 BOOKS
AND A SURPRISE GIFT!

We would like to take this opportunity to thank you for reading this Mills & Boon® book by offering you the chance to take FOUR more specially selected titles from the Presents...™ series absolutely FREE! We're also making this offer to introduce you to the benefits of the Reader Service™ —

★ FREE home delivery   ★ FREE gifts and competitions
★ FREE monthly Newsletter   ★ Exclusive Reader Service discounts
★ Books available before they're in the shops

Accepting these FREE books and gift places you under no obligation to buy; you may cancel at any time, even after receiving your free shipment. Simply complete your details below and return the entire page to the address below. *You don't even need a stamp!*

YES! Please send me 4 free Presents...™ books and a surprise gift. I understand that unless you hear from me, I will receive 6 superb new titles every month for just £2.40 each, postage and packing free. I am under no obligation to purchase any books and may cancel my subscription at any time. The free books and gift will be mine to keep in any case. POEC

Ms/Mrs/Miss/Mr ....Initials ....
BLOCK CAPITALS PLEASE

Surname ....

Address ....

....

....Postcode ....

Send this whole page to:
UK: FREEPOST CN81, Croydon, CR9 3WZ
EIRE: PO Box 4546, Kilcock, County Kildare (stamp required)

Offer valid in UK and Eire only and not available to current Reader Service subscribers to this series. We reserve the right to refuse an application and applicants must be aged 18 years or over. Only one application per household. Terms and prices subject to change without notice. Offer expires 31st December 2000. As a result of this application, you may receive further offers from Harlequin Mills & Boon Limited and other carefully selected companies. If you would prefer not to share in this opportunity please write to The Data Manager at the address above.

Mills & Boon® is a registered trademark owned by Harlequin Mills & Boon Limited.
Presents...™ is being used as a trademark.